A

CANDLELIGHT REGENCY SPECIAL

REGENCY ROMANCES BY JANET LOUISE ROBERTS

A MARRIAGE OF INCONVENIENCE
THE DANCING DOLL
THE GOLDEN THISTLE
LA CASA DORADA
THE CARDROSS LUCK
THE FIRST WALTZ

MY LADY MISCHIEF

Janet Louise Roberts

A CANDLELIGHT REGENCY SPECIAL

Published by
Dell Publishing Co., Inc.
1 Dag Hammarskjold Plaza
New York, New York 10017

ISBN: 0-440-16228-9

Printed in Canada

Previous Dell Edition #6228
New Dell Edition
First printing—July 1978

MY LADY MISCHIEF

CHAPTER ONE

ALL THAT GRAY April day, Mary Margaret MacGregor had been eagerly leaning forward in the clumsy, swaying coach, surveying the Cornish countryside. Now in mid-afternoon, as dusk was falling, she was too weary to gaze out anymore. She had been traveling for most of two days, in the chill spring weather, and she felt cold, miserable, and apprehensive.

She kept thinking to herself, the more her bones ached and her head hurt, "What a foolish girl I am, to be sure!" She had thrown over a "good" job, though her lip curled sarcastically at the thought of it. She had flung everything to the four winds, and taken off on this long coach journey—to marry a man she scarcely knew in a land she had never seen.

She leaned back with a little sigh, grateful to finally be alone in the coach. The last farmer had left a dozen villages back. She could stretch out her legs, push back the gray bonnet sitting so demurely on her fiery red hair, and yawn and think and brood to her heart's content about the past years.

Her parents had died of the fever when she was twelve.

She had left school, and had had the "good fortune" to be a maid and then a governess in the large Everton family. As the family had increased to its present size of nine children, ranging in age from eighteen down to two, with another baby coming, the more valuable Mary's services had become—not in wages, but in imperious demands for attention.

She smiled in amusement as she recalled the dismay of Robin and Lucinda Everton when they finally realized at the end that the maid, the governess, the companion, the housekeeper, the fill-in-at-everything was leaving them.

"But you have been happy here! And we promised to give you a home for life," wailed Mrs. Everton, rocking the smallest one automatically after Mary had given him back to his mother.

"I am going to be wed," said Mary, scarcely believing it herself.

"You hardly know the boy!" said Mr. Everton severely. "Ask him to come and visit you again. This is much too suddenly prepared! It is unseemly."

Mary had pushed her red hair back from her face, surveying the two of them with the quick humor that seldom deserted her.

"He says he's a viscount," she said, cheerfully. "Well, that's to be seen. He does live in a castle, so there's an interesting change. I'll find out what I find out when I get there. It isn't as though we were married yet. I can always change my mind."

"And come back to us," said Mrs. Everton quickly. "Though, I warn you, Mary, we might have another girl by that time. This is a fine post, and you must admit we have been good to you."

Mary was silent, her face shadowing. She could not force her reluctant, honest tongue to say that they had been good to her. She had worked hard since the day she had come ten years ago, at the age of twelve—a few days off during the year, some reluctantly given shillings, cross words, work from five in the morning until midnight at times, and even later when a child was ill, which frequently happened. She was weary to her fine bones.

"You are an ungrateful, reckless, foolish girl," Mr. Everton finally pronounced, when they saw she was set on leaving. "And do *not* expect to return to us! We shall hire someone else immediately, preferably an older woman who will not be so unreliable!"

That did sting. Mary opened her mouth to protest, then shut it again in a hard line. She had faithfully performed all the duties required of her, and some had been bitter. As she had come of age and reached an attractive maturity, she had been hidden deliberately in the nursery so she would not outshine the dull, plain Everton girls at their parties. No longer was she required to act as maid at the balls. She had only to look in the mirror and compare her slim, rounded figure and flaming red-gold curls with the plumpness, bad complexions, and mouse-brown hair of the Everton girls to know why.

How she had had the good fortune to meet young Christopher Huntingdon, Viscount Courtley, and find time to meet him in the gardens twice, she would never know. But it had happened. He had gazed at her with awed admiration, professed his love, reverently kissed her hand, and vowed to return soon to fetch her to his home. He had not left without proposing to her, and she had accepted him, scarcely believing it was true.

Long weeks had elapsed, during which she thought bitterly that he had forgotten her. Then the incredible, precious letter arrived, and the plump packet of money with it. He had written saying that he could not come, but that she must come to him, and he had sent ten guineas to help pay for the journey. She had not hesitated, but had given notice at once.

Anything, anything to leave this rough, hard work, this

ungrateful occupation which seemed to stretch drearily forward through the years to a faded ending in the same household. Always in demand, always ordered about, never really wanted for herself or her warm heart, only for her quick hands and quicker mind.

To be loved, she thought longingly, to be loved! She had not been loved by anyone since the days of her parents' death. Never loved, though her heart ached for it, and her eyes stung with tears. She felt empty, though her life was busy, busy, busy.

Then Christopher had loved her. His eyes had glowed when he looked at her. His hands had touched her reverently, his kiss had stung her little red, worn hand. He would love her and protect her, give her a home. A castle? She did not care if it turned out to be a cottage! Only to be wanted, needed, protected, and loved.

The coach pulled up with a jerk and protests from the weary horses. Someone opened the door and let down the steps. She climbed out stiffly and looked about. It was yet another village of white-and-black-striped stores and houses, stuccoed and trim. The inn yard seemed clean and neat; the innkeeper wore a fresh blue apron and a brisk manner.

He came up to her and helped her with her worn traveling bag and carpetbag. "Where would ye be going, miss?" he asked courteously, with a quick, keen look at her face.

"To the Castle of St. John, sir," she said, wearily. "Is there someone here to meet me?"

"The castle? Nobody here from the castle, miss. Be it today ye was arriving?"

"Yes, I wrote. Maybe they didn't receive my letter."

He thought about it. "Ah, well. Mr. Jones the grocer be sending supplies up there this late afternoon. He would be taking you with him in his wagon, if that pleases you."

Just to get there, just to rest in Christopher's arms and be reassured, she thought.

"Yes, sir, it would be kind of him, and you are kind to suggest it," she said, politely.

He smiled down at her from his great height and nodded. It was arranged, and in an hour the grocer came for her, and took her up on the wagon seat with him. It was chilly and rainy; Mary huddled further into her damp cloak and wished miserably that she had never come. Why had Christopher not met her? Why had he not come to fetch her himself? Was he ill or injured? He rode so recklessly, perhaps he had broken his leg, though he had not mentioned it. Was she really a very foolish girl, to come like this without assurances?

She had been desperate indeed, she thought. Another year, another month, another day, in the chaotic Everton household, running at everyone's bidding, no moment to call her own, rushing from feeding the baby to hearing the eldest boy's lessons, to tying the sash for the oldest, snobbish girl for her ball, to washing out the linens when the linen maid was ill. And always shunted aside, hidden away from the company.

She had grabbed at the chance to leave; grabbed at it and escaped as wildly as her own Scottish ancestor had escaped after his capture by the English during a battle. He had gnawed through the ropes that bound him, slipped past the sleeping guard, and crawled up a mountain into the snow and ice with his feet bleeding and his boots gone, to hide out like an animal for two months before they gave up the search for him. They had told his story proudly in her family; she had heard it many a time at her father's knee.

"And Mary Margaret, my dear," her father would always conclude, with his red head held high, "your grandfather never walked again without a limp, but he was a free man. Free. And freedom is worth all the sacrifice and trials in the whole world."

"Ah, yes indeed it is, Father," she whispered to herself.

But was she going from one bondage to another? That she did not know. She gazed across the Cornish moors, the desolate rocks and wastelands, the few clumps of green, the rainy, wind-swept wilds, and knew fear. But she was a Scot; she had her pride and her mind. She would make do and manage somehow.

Mr. Jones, the grocer, was a kind though silent man. When he had driven up the steep hill to the top, he pointed with his whip. "There be the castle. I'll take you around to the front first, miss. Ye'll want to go in the front, as ye are quality."

With that he lapsed into silence again. Her heart full, she gazed at her future home. The Castle of St. John loomed on the hill like a fortress of gray stone and red brick, with turrets and mossy towers, and huge windows which gaped in the late afternoon like dull gray eyes. The grimness of the castle was contrasted with the huge gardens that surrounded it. The aged moat had been converted into a flower bed which rioted with spring blossoms of red and pink and yellow.

As the grocer drove up to the huge entrance and clattered across the plank drawbridge—which was down permanently, it seemed, for the ropes were covered with green moss—he pointed to the huge wooden doors. "From the time of Her Majesty Elizabeth," he said. "Earlier ones burned in. Family fought them off. Won."

"Oh," said Mary.

"Didn't like the English much in these parts," said Mr. Jones, "as we be more Welsh. Ye be English?" He gave a timid glance at her, especially at her red hair.

"Scottish, I am," she said, proudly.

"Right," he said, nodding with satisfaction as he drew up at the front gate. The door opened silently and a gray-haired man came out, looking up at them. "Lady be here for you, Mr. Wenrick," said the grocer briskly.

Mr. Wenrick helped Mary down from the wagon, then motioned to the footman behind him to take her luggage. No surprise showed in his smoothshaven face. But the footman could not repress his wide-eyed amazement.

Mr. Wenrick, the butler, showed her in most courteously, and took her to a small, stiff front parlor beyond the wide and gracious hall. He returned in minutes with Mrs. Ramsey, the housekeeper, a woman seemingly in her thirties, smart-looking and keen.

"Yes, miss? Did you wish to apply for a post here?" asked the woman briskly, her gaze moving from Mary's head of gray bonnet and red curls to her shabby gray skirts.

Mary lifted her chin. "I wish to see Christopher Huntingdon, Viscount Courtley," she said proudly. "He has sent for me to come to him. We are to be married."

There was a long silence. The housekeeper stared at her, then vacantly at some distant point. "Ah—yes, miss," she said, colorlessly. "Sir Christopher is not in at present. His brother, Lord Stephen Huntingdon, the Lord St. John, will see you when he returns, I am sure. Meantime, allow me to get you some tea. You have had a long journey?"

"Two days," said Mary, with a sigh she could not suppress. "And I am so tired—tea would be most welcome."

The housekeeper smiled at her compassionately, and said, "There, now, let me help you off with your cloak and bonnet. You'll like a bit of a wash, I expect. Come this way, miss—ah—"

"Mary Margaret MacGregor," said Mary.

"Miss MacGregor. And Scottish, I think, yes, miss?" And the housekeeper led her into another room. She washed and felt somewhat better.

Then Mrs. Ramsey took her back to the small, stiff parlor, where a maid in a black dress and white cuffs was laying out an immense tea. The pot was of white porcelain with beautiful pink roses and blue trim. The matching cups were dainty but full-sized, holding large amounts of tea. The bread and butter was cut into dainty sandwiches, and there were plates of ham, cold beef, and cheeses. Mrs. Ramsey left it with her and withdrew, and Mary immediately began eating with a great appetite.

The tea, which was really a good supper, restored her spirits and her courage. Her weary body relaxed in the blue satin slipper chair, and her eyes were refreshed by the beautiful art objects in the small, stiff, yet lovely room. There was a portrait on the wall of a blonde-haired woman with kind brown eyes, dating to about two hundred years before. On the white mantel were several small objects which she was too weary to examine, two statuettes of Greek gods, a miniature tower of wood, an alabaster egg precariously resting in a wooden holder, and an ancient pewter mug with interesting dents in it.

On the wall hung a small collection of weapons, a battle-ax with a battered handle, a dented shield whose crest of letters was so worn as to be unreadable, and a faded battle flag on its standard of warped wood.

It was a very old place, mused Mary. It must be as ancient as some of the Scottish castles of her childhood days, the places whose names and histories her father had proudly recited to her. So Christopher came from a proud old family. Perhaps they had lost their money; that might account for his odd behavior toward her. He might be afraid she would scorn him. Oh, no, she thought, she would love him even for just the fact that he had rescued her from terrible drudgery and humiliating circumstances.

The door opened as she was half-drowsing beside the warm fire, feeling more comfortable than she had felt for two days. She started up as Mrs. Ramsey entered.

"My lord will see you now, Miss MacGregor. He awaits you in his study," she said, seeming more formal than before.

"Thank you," replied Mary, and allowed the woman to show her down the hall to the side of the huge wing. They seemed to walk for a long distance, past ancestral portraits and battle flags, weapons, sideboards of shining cherry wood, and a wide staircase, past glimpses of drawing rooms and parlors and a dining room set in white linen for an elaborate dinner. She was struck with a sense of dismay as she saw it. She had begun to picture Christopher as a gallant, poverty-stricken viscount. But now this house did not look like that of a poor but noble family. It seemed most elaborate and wealthy.

Mrs. Ramsey opened a door of shining dark wood, led Mary inside, and shut the door firmly behind them. They walked across acres of soft, thick Persian carpets of cream, green, and rose to the huge desk at one side. The man sitting in the large chair rose to his feet and stood behind the desk, looking at Mary with the coldest sherry-colored brown eyes she had ever seen.

It was his eyes she saw first, for they commanded and compelled before he spoke even a word. Then she noticed the long irregular scar on his left cheek, running from forehead to chin. He was deeply tanned. From the sea? she wondered. He was about six feet tall and seemed to tower over her five feet four inches, even from across the desk. He waved an immaculate hand at a chair, and she seated herself on the edge of the red satin slipper chair across from him.

"Miss MacGregor," he said, and his voice was so deep and powerful that she jumped slightly. "That will be all, Mrs. Ramsey. I will ring."

The housekeeper left the room silently. The lord remained standing, staring down at Mary. She lifted her small chin and returned his glare in full measure. Her courage had returned, and she wanted some answers. Such as, why was Christopher not here to meet her? Why had she not been met by the carriage at the village? Why was she being received so coldly by the lord? And who was he?

He answered her last question as though reading her mind.

"I am Stephen Huntingdon, Lord St. John. My brother is Christopher Huntingdon. I believe you have business with him."

"Ye may call it business," said Mary, her Scottish accent flaring as it did when she was angry. "He has asked me to marry him, and I am come to do just that. Why is he not here to meet me?"

The lord stared down his long Roman nose at her. She stared right back, her green eyes flashing. "Christopher—is not here at present," he said slowly. "I find it difficult to believe he is going to marry you. You are—I presume—a maid—or a governess?"

She flushed because he had characterized her so accurately. "A governess, sir, and a maid, and a nursery girl, and many other duties did I perform for the Everton family, where I met Christopher," she informed him coldly, her chin up high. "When he wrote and asked me to marry him, I wrote back that I would come. That is the full of it."

Now he sat down, slowly, thoughtfully, still staring at her with a little frown which did little to detract from his formidable appearance. He was in his early thirties, she judged, and used to being obeyed. She wondered why Christopher had not mentioned his brother.

"I find this difficult to believe, Miss MacGregor," he said, and she knew he was being formal and coldly sarcastic on purpose. "You see, my brother is on his honeymoon. He was married two days ago to Miss Georgiana Demerest."

The words came to Mary as though from a great distance, as though the sea roared in her ears, as though someone pounded on her head with a huge hammer. She stared at him but did not see him, for she felt dizzy and faint. Married. She could not believe it.

"Are you faint, miss?" he asked curtly, half-rising. "I will get some hartshorn. Are you in the—family way, miss?" And he reached for a small gold vessel on the table, as though to hand it to her.

She stiffened at the insult. "No, sir, I have not been having familiar relations with your brother. He asked me to marry him! He did not have an—an improper relation with me!" And she glared at the man furiously. "I did not come here to be insulted. I came to marry Christopher, as he asked me to do!"

He sighed, as though at a child who had wilfully misunderstood him. "I have told you, miss," he said very curtly, moving some papers as though impatient to return to more important matters, "he is married. To Georgiana Demerest, the only daughter of the local squire. They were married two days ago, and are off on their wedding journey. I do not expect them back for some weeks. I find it quite difficult to believe he meant to marry you. What do you want from us?"

She was so angry, incredulous, heartsick, that she could scarcely comprehend what he said. All she knew was that he was insulting her. He had asked if she was expecting a child; now he thought she had come to demand money. Without answering him, she opened her faded reticule and fumbled inside. She found the two letters Christopher had written to her and took them out. They were worn from much rereading. Those two precious letters which she had imagined meant freedom from a life of humiliation and slavery.

She handed them across the wide table. "The letters he wrote to me," she said curtly. She watched his face as he opened the letters and read them quite slowly and deliberately, his nostrils flaring.

She would not have imagined it. He was deeply shocked. He read the letters a second time before folding them and returning them to her. A flush began to rise in his tanned face, tinting the high cheekbones. His sherry-brown eyes warmed, and were troubled.

"My brother—my half brother, I should say—seems to have misled you, Miss MacGregor," he said, sounding human for the first time. "I imagine he wrote you at a time when he and his fiancée had had some sort of lover's tiff. But the way he wrote—you could be excused for believing he was sincere."

"Thank you, sir," and now it was she who was sarcastic. "I am so pleased you finally believe me!"

"Yes. Let me think. I shall supply you with funds, and after you have rested, you will return to your home and—"

"No," she said sharply, and with keen distaste. "I shall never return to the Evertons. I have no home there. My parents have been dead many years. I was worked like a slave. I shall not return to them!"

Now he looked at her as though seeing her for the first time, the proud red head, the uplifted chin, the troubled green eyes. He saw the work-worn hands clutched on the reticule, the mended gray dusty gown, the pallor of the weary face.

His tone gentled. "I must rectify this—error," he said. "I will think what to do to make it up to you, this foolishness of Christopher's. He is always up to some mischief, I fear," he added, rather apologetically. "He is quite young. You must stay here a few days and rest. Then, if you will, I shall send you to London, give you references, and help you obtain a new post, something you will like better than your recent employment." He rose, indicating the end of their meeting, and rang a bell. Mrs. Ramsey entered so promptly that Mary knew she had been waiting in the hall.

"Yes, my lord?" asked the housekeeper.

Mary rose also, uncertainly. She felt weak and nauseous, and heartsick at the deception so cruelly and casually practiced on her.

"You will show Miss MacGregor to a bedroom, and give her every attention. She shall be our guest for several days until she proceeds to London," said the lord, and waved his hand casually to dismiss them. He returned to his huge desk and the papers on it.

Mrs. Ramsey hesitated. "What room shall I prepare for her, sir?"

"Ah—room. Yes. Well—the jade bedroom. It will match her eyes," he said drily, glancing once at Mary. She disliked the half-smile more than the cold sarcasm he had shown her before.

They left the room. Mary was burning, half with weariness and a slight fever and half with fury. Christopher—how could he do this to her? Was it true? Well, in the next few days she would discover for herself. She could not believe anyone could be as cruel as the men in this family!

CHAPTER TWO

THE HOUSEKEEPER, in a black satin gown, led the way up the wide staircase. The red carpet hushed their footsteps, and Mary wanted to pause at each landing to rest. She would also have liked to examine the many Greek statues on the landings, and the portraits hanging on the walls.

But Mrs. Ramsey went briskly onward. At the top of the stairway, she turned to the left, and strode along the long hall to the last room at the end.

She opened a door, and Mary, following her, gasped in surprise. She had thought she would be put in a poor, nondescript room, suitable for "governesses and maids"; instead, she seemed to be in a grand guest room.

"This is the jade bedroom, miss," said Mrs. Ramsey. "Your bathroom is beyond, I will show you. Also, there is a grand vista of the gardens and the sea. I hope it will please you."

The woman's kindness and evident concern did much to soothe Mary's ruffled feelings. She set down her cloak and bonnet, and went obediently to survey the view from the tall French windows.

She drew a deep breath as she looked. Beyond the window were acres of the most beautiful formal gardens she had ever seen. They exceeded in size and elaborateness any gardens she had ever viewed, including those at the castle of the squire who lived near the Evertons.

The box hedges stretched down and down toward the distant sea, which rumbled and crashed against gray cliffs. The sea was darkly blue now and only dimly visible in the last glows of the sunset that held back the darkness. She would be able to gaze out the next day and see the gardens in their fully radiant spring glory, the greens of the hedges and massive trees, the small artificial lake, the white gazebo she could just make out. And beyond—the glorious sea.

She turned back into the room with a little sigh of pleasure. She did not know what was going to happen to her, but for now she would take delight in her surroundings. The housekeeper was watching her with a slight frown, but it relaxed into a smile as she saw Mary's pleasure.

"Lovely, is it not? I could scarce believe it myself when I was fresh down from London last year," said the young woman impulsively. Then she caught herself. "You may wish to rest for two hours, Miss MacGregor. I will send your maid, Bonny, to you at the end of that time. Dinner will be in the formal dining room at 8 P.M."

After the woman had left, Mary removed her dusty shoes, then cast herself down wearily on the huge bed and began to examine the room. The walls were of jade green wallpaper overlaid with a delicate pattern of sprays of mossy green and gray. Her bed was huge, with an elaborate canopy of jade green silk trimmed with long gold ropes, and belonged to the previous century.

The other furnishings were simpler, but beautiful. Carved wood chairs with seats of gold satin, a long gold chaise longue, carved wood dresser, and tall wardrobe. On a small table near the bed were a lamp and candle, several little porcelain dishes, and an alabaster box trimmed with gold. She looked from one thing to another, examining all with the delighted curiosity of a child turned loose in a museum.

And she had thought Christopher might live in a cottage. She winced at the thought of him and turned her face into the satin pillow. He had hurt her badly. Why had he treated her so? Or could they be lying to her? Had they learned of his intentions to marry her and resolved to keep them apart? She must use her wits, she decided. At dinner, she might be able to learn something.

At the appointed time, a thin, nervous girl of about nineteen or twenty, who identified herself as Bonny, came to her room to attend her.

Bonny was evidently a village girl being trained for the household, and was quite nervous and silent in her anxiety to please. Mary was able to relax with her, and did not feel so ashamed of her shabby dresses. But it was an effort to decide what to wear. She finally chose her shabby good black dress, a hand-me-down from Mrs. Everton herself, which had been taken in two sizes.

With it, she wore the only piece of jewelry she owned, a pin of Scottish design with her mother's crest on it. She touched it longingly. If only it would give her the courage to proceed!

Bonny showed her down to the living room where two people awaited her. One was the lord of St. John, strikingly attractive in a formal coat of crimson velvet, rubies at his throat and on his finger. The other was a thin, nervous blonde woman in an elaborate gown of chiffon and silk, as blue as her eyes. Mary thought she must be the wife of Lord Stephen Huntingdon.

The lord stood up promptly as Mary entered, showing his good manners. She advanced slowly toward them across the mile of Aubusson carpet, only dimly aware of the beauty of the cream-colored pile under her feet, the creamy walls, the blue silk fabrics, the white woodwork.

"Ah, Miss MacGregor. Mother, may I present to you Miss Mary Margaret MacGregor. Miss MacGregor, this is Lady Helena Huntingdon, the mother of Viscount Courtley, whom you have met."

Curiosity flickered in the eyes of Lady Helena. Mary understood at once the woman had not been told of the circumstances of her arrival. She held out a languid hand for Mary to touch briefly, stared at the black gown with a droop of her lip, and said, "How lovely to meet you. Where did you meet my son?"

"At the home of the Everton family," she said briefly. Lord Stephen interrupted, as if he were afraid she was going to speak further.

"I believe our dinner is ready, if we may go in, Mother." He took Lady Helena in on his arm, leaving Mary to trail them. He seated Mary on his left, Lady Helena on his right, at the end of an elaborate long table in an enormous room. She felt as though they were the only guests who had arrived of an expected hundred or so!

Mary did not have to say much, for Lady Helena chattered on and on, foolishly, ramblingly, as though accustomed to monopolizing the conversation. She spoke of the gardens, of her disappointing trip to see the vicar's wife in the village, of her disapproval of the goings-on of the young people of today, of the dullness now that the wedding was over.

She turned unexpectedly to Mary at that. "I suppose you came for the wedding and arrived too late. How sad. It was a lively affair, I assure you! All the world came down from London, and we had a hundred guests here all week."

"Forty, Mother," corrected Stephen, in his deep, indifferent tone, and snapped his fingers at the footman to remove the plates.

"You did come for the wedding, Miss MacGregor," persisted Lady Helena.

"I came for a wedding, yes," said Mary, and looked deliberately at Lord St. John. She surprised a rising flush on his cheeks, and he changed the subject to the gardens, asking his stepmother what she meant to plant in the moat this summer.

After the long elaborate dinner, with wines which Mary refused, they went into a smaller drawing room. Lady Helena relaxed on a long couch and beckoned Mary to sit beside her. Lord Stephen, after a pause which showed unusual uncertainty for him, came to sit near them.

Lady Helena chattered on and on about the wedding. It was evidently the biggest event of many a year for her. If Stephen Huntingdon had tried, he could not have found more convincing proof that his half brother had really been married, for Lady Helena was full of the most minute details.

She described the gown of dear Georgiana, the white veil, the going-away outfit, where they were going on the wedding journey—"to Bath, my dear, if you can credit it! Georgiana wished to go to Bath, though Christopher wanted to go to London, but he gave the dear bride her wish. But if he means to go on this way and spoil the girl, I am sure she will rule him forever. Though she adores my dear boy, and I am sure she means to obey him and let him be lord, which is as it should be. Such a dear girl. I am so happy for my son."

Mary asked one question. "How soon do they mean to return from their wedding journey, ma'am?"

"Oh, not for some weeks," said Lady Helena, vaguely, and began to recall her own wedding journey years before, and how sick she had been when her dear lord had insisted on a Channel journey across to Paris. "Though I did love dear Paris, it was so sweet and pretty."

Mary glanced at Lord St. John and found him watching her keenly under his half-closed lids. The sherry-brown eyes could be sharp and discerning, she learned.

"Your own wedding, dear Stephen, would have been even more elegant," said Lady Helena, suddenly, switching from the gaieties of Paris. "If only dear Angela had lived! Everyone loved the girl. They had planned the most elaborate fête, my dear Miss MacGregor! All the countryside was invited."

Mary started. She had been watching Stephen's face, and as his stepmother said the words, she had seen the change that came over it. A sudden, intense change, a sadness, a rage, a fury, a strangeness; the sherry-brown eyes opened wide, then closed tight, and his mouth twisted in an intense fury. Such a mixture of emotions that Mary was quite shocked.

Lady Helena touched Mary's arm and drew her attention to a lovely portrait on a side wall. "There is dear Angela —Angela Tarrant, such a beautiful girl." Mary stared up at the portrait of the lovely blonde girl, whose intelligent blue eyes stared straight out. She wore a glorious blue gown of the most fragile fabric, which drifted about her white shoulders like a piece of heaven come to rest for a moment. The full-length portrait showed her slim figure, tiny waist, long, delicate hands holding flowers. She appeared tall, regal, yet of a gentleness and beauty that caught and held one's attention.

"What happened to her?" asked Mary involuntarily, and looked at Stephen. He had opened his eyes finally and was staring up at the portrait with a mixture of regret, anger, and something else she could not identify.

"She died," he said, briefly, and stood up. "Miss MacGregor, you must be very weary. I will ring for the footman to show you to your room."

"Just a few days before the wedding," said Lady Helena. "Oh, dear, such a sweet girl, and so very smart, and such a good nature. And to die like that—"

"Enough!" said Stephen, and rang for the footman. His face had turned tight and hard, and if not for his tan,

Mary thought, he would have been white. His cheeks had lost that tinge of red on the cheekbones. As he waited, he put his big hands behind his back.

He wished her goodnight very coldly, and after she had left the room, she could hear him say to Lady Helena, "I wish you would not speak of that! You know I dislike it!"

"Oh, dear, but my dear boy, it was a year ago, more than a year ago. Very well, I shall not—"

At breakfast the next morning, after a long, exhausted sleep, Mary met another member of the strange household, evidently a temporarily remaining member of the wedding party.

Young Mr. Lance Tarrant, Viscount Greville, introduced himself to Mary, since they were the first ones in the breakfast room. Over kippers and sausage, he told her his life history quite freely. She listened to the young blond man with great fascination.

"My sister Angela was the most beautiful woman in the world," he told her finally, and suddenly she realized why the name was familiar.

"Oh, yes, she was to have married Lord St. John," said Mary, forgetting her tea for a moment. "Her portrait hangs in the blue drawing room—"

"Yes. It was so dreadful! I discovered her in the gardens, you see," he said, and for a moment, he seemed not a polite, poised young man, but an anguished human being. "Angela—terribly bloody, her throat cut—"

Mary put her own hand involuntarily to her throat. "Her—throat—cut—?" she asked in a strangled tone. She stared at the fashionably dressed young man in frock coat and wide white stock.

"Yes. Murdered. No one knew why or how, or who had done it. We never found out." He put his long white hand over his face, and slowly drew it down, as though reassuming a mask. "But I'm not supposed to speak of it," he added dully. "Stephen dislikes it dreadfully."

"But I'm quite—interested," said Mary. She was determined to know more about the strange Lord St. John, who ruled this castle with the same iron hand which his ancestors had evidently used to keep out the English hundreds of years before. "Do tell me—were there no clues, was there no evidence?"

"I'll show you the place I found her after breakfast," he said, with gloomy satisfaction. "I'll tell you all about it—only don't tell Stephen. He dislikes it, and berates me if I speak of it."

Just then Stephen and Lady Helena, entered with several others, also stragglers from the wedding party, Mary learned, as they were introduced. They took it for granted that she had come for the wedding and arrived too late. As indeed, said one guest, a lady from London, it was planned so very suddenly, only a month's notice.

Lance lapsed into what was evidently his customary silence, and Mary also was silent, sitting in her faded, tight blue dress from three years ago, very much aware of her shabbiness among the elaborate toilettes of the other ladies present.

After breakfast, Lance took her out to the gardens. Stephen watched them depart with a slight frown, but made no move to stop them. Lance walked along rapidly, past views and plots and flowers where she would have lingered. "No, no, it was down near the cliffs," he said impatiently, "near the sea."

As they walked, Lance described vividly how he had found the body of his dead sister. Mary was already shuddering with horror when they arrived near the spot.

"Now, it was over there, just there—near that scrub of a tree—oh, my God! She's there now!" the young man cried out, and covered his face in horror.

Mary took another step forward, and another. "No," she said, in a small voice. "It's—a dog. He's—dead."

Lance shuddered, tried to recover, and went forward to look. "My God—it's Commander," he said. He stood up, his hand bloody from touching the animal, his thin face white and strained. "It's Stephen's favorite dog! My God. Why would anyone kill a dog?"

They returned to the castle, and Mary escaped to her bedroom while Lance went to inform Stephen of the mishap. Mary watched from her bedroom windows, looking out over the glorious vista of gardens and sea, while men tramped back and forth along the flower beds and white cliffs, looking about them. Someone covered and wrapped the body of the large guard dog, and carried it away. Still she watched.

She felt tired and feverish. Too much was happening all at once, after the long dullness of her years as a governess. She thought of returning to the life she had known, and shuddered. The cruelty of young Christopher Huntingdon had shocked her profoundly. He had sent for her even as he was preparing his own wedding, inviting guests from London, and his bride was having her elaborate gown stitched! What kind of man was he, really, and what kind of man was his half brother Stephen?

Both seemed cold and cruel, with a thick overlay of deceiving charm. She wondered why Angela Tarrant had been murdered, and who had done it. Could it have been Stephen himself? Was that why he would not permit the topic to be mentioned in his presence?

She watched as the dog was removed and the men left. Finally, the scene was empty of people again, and its beauty shone in the late morning sun.

She rested for a while, then wakened feeling both feverish and chilly. The room was warm enough. She must have caught a chill, she thought, on that long, rainy journey.

She shivered again, and finally put on a warm wool

plaid which had been her mother's. The tartan was the Bruce design, wide green with narrow gold and white lines. It comforted and warmed her; and she put on the brooch also.

At lunch, she sat silently while the guests gossiped and reluctantly discussed in an idle way the thought of returning to their own homes. Stephen Huntingdon was polite to them but distant, as though he secretly wished they would leave.

Mary rested again in the afternoon, and slept soundly. But she wakened feeling even worse—hot and feverish and chilled all at once. She had a slight cough which she tried to conceal when she spoke to the maid, but the village girl said, "I'll bring you some hot tea with honey and lemon. That will help you, miss."

Mary welcomed the attentions, but she was afraid she was in for a spell of fever. She was run-down from the past years of eating very little, running from one duty to another. Now she was relaxed, and exhausted, and her strength seemed quite depleted.

She retired early that night after dinner, timidly refusing a game of whist and noticing that no one seemed grieved at her departure. She left feeling there was no one in the world who cared in the slightest whether she was in the world or not. Even Commander, the dog, had aroused more attention than she did, she thought bitterly.

Mary felt quite sorry for herself that night. She even cried a little before she went to sleep, which was most unusual for her. She had a strong, determined disposition, and generally nothing could get her down for long. Her sense of humor would come to the rescue.

At breakfast the next morning, she found Lord St. John there ahead of her. He approached her as she entered the room and spoke in a low tone, though only footmen were in the large breakfast room.

"I would like to see you in my study after breakfast, Miss MacGregor."

"Yes, sir," she said, automatically.

Then Lance Tarrant came in, and his face lit up when he saw her. "Ah, Miss Mary, you are early this morning," he said cheerfully. They chatted amiably during their tea and sausage and cakes, and she found some pleasure in the fact that Stephen scowled at them several times during the meal.

None of the others came to breakfast while they were there. After they had eaten, Mary meekly followed Lord Stephen to his study. He opened the door for her, stood aside for her to enter, then shut the door decidedly behind them. He motioned her to the chair opposite his desk, and she sat down while he went behind the desk to sit in the huge armchair.

"Ah, yes," he said absently, and shuffled some papers. "Miss MacGregor, some of the guests are proceeding to London the day after tomorrow. I thought you might accompany them in one of my carriages. I will write out some letters of recommendation for you. If you will inform me of the exact nature of the duties you have performed—"

She answered his businesslike questions with growing bitterness. She had expected by this time to be a cherished and protected wife. Instead, she would have to go back into service, become a governess, and a slave, for someone she did not know. Another stranger, who would bully her and push her about. A service from early morning to late at night.

She felt feverish and pushed her red hair back impatiently from her warm forehead.

"You might like London," he said impersonally, not looking up from where his pen scribbled busily on a large white sheet of paper. "You might take service in one of the grand households there. They will pay considerably more than what you have been paid."

She bit her lip. She had been paid so little that if Christopher had not sent her ten guineas, she would not have been able to come in the coach. All her anguish, hurt, and humiliation seemed to well up in her.

"Oh, sir, I expect I shall be able to receive considerable pay," she snapped, so sharply that his head came up and the sherry-brown eyes surveyed her in some surprise. "I expect to visit an attorney soon after I arrive in London."

"An attorney," he said, and laid down the pen. His big hands folded on the desk, and he fixed his gaze on her ominously. She did not take fright. Her small chin came up, and she glared back at him as she had done on her arrival.

"Yes, sir. I have heard there is much interest in London when a man promises marriage and deceives a poor working girl, and then deserts her. I have the two letters, you know."

There was a long silence in the room. He stared at her, the red touching his cheekbones, and his eyes hard and furious. Her green eyes glared right back, though she was twisting her hands in her lap.

"You would—bring suit—in court," he said, slowly.

She did not know all the procedure. All she had heard was backstairs gossip when a girl had been made pregnant by a friend of Mr. Everton, and the case had been in the gazettes. But it sounded right.

"Yes, my lord. I would bring suit. It would be in the gazettes, how he treated me." She felt dizzy, as though she were about to faint, but she persisted. "He promised me marriage. He sent for me. I want what I came for! Not a governess post in some strange house where they could beat me if they liked!"

"Did the Evertons beat you?" he asked, his tone cold.

"Yes, sir, when I was younger. Until I learned to curb my Scottish tongue."

"I see. Well—Miss MacGregor. What if I offered you a post in this household? You could be governess here. Of course, your services would not be required much at present, but eventually, I suppose, there would be children—a lifetime post—"

But even the Lord St. John seemed to realize how strange it would be if Mary accepted a post as governess in a home where the children she would teach would belong to the man she had expected to marry.

"No, sir, not that. I would not be governess for Christopher's children," she said, with a toss of her curly red hair. Her green eyes blazed at him. "What do you think of me? Do you think I would meekly live here under his roof, taking care of his children, when I thought to live with him as his wife?"

He studied her, his mouth thoughtful, his eyes distant. He seemed not so much to see her as to see through her, she thought, irritated.

Finally he spoke. "You have—good breeding," he said, oddly. "You are—or could be—beautiful, in the right clothing, with the right care. Very well. What if I offered you another marriage—one just as fine, or better? What if I offered to marry you myself?"

She thought he spoke sarcastically, to test her, and she flushed deeply, angrily. "Oh, sir, I should accept at once, of course," she said, bitingly. "I could not turn down such an honor! You overwhelm me—"

To her surprise, and some horror, she saw him rising. His face was expressionless, but she thought she recognized anger. His eyes were as hard as marble.

"Very well, then. You accept me. I have offered you marriage, and you have accepted. Shall we inform my guests? Our guests? Perhaps the ones returning to London will consent to stay and be witnesses. For we shall marry at once, I think," he said, and came around the desk to her.

She stared up at him, paralyzed. She could not move or speak as he took her small round chin in his hand. And he bent down from his great height and touched her mouth with his firm lips.

When he kissed her, she knew he was furiously, terribly angry, but maintaining full control of himself, his fingers tight, his lips scarcely moving on hers.

CHAPTER THREE

MARY STOOD GAZING at her reflection in the mirror as Mrs. Ramsey adjusted the long white satin dress. She did not recognize herself.

The past two days had gone by in a feverish daze. She had tried to explain to Lord Stephen that she had thought he was joking, that she did not mean to marry him, that she would go on to London. He would hear nothing of it.

He had presented her to his guests and his stepmother as his future wife. They had all been deeply shocked, gossipy, and excited, speculating in low tones even in her presence. Stephen, furiously angry, had turned colder and more haughty.

Mrs. Ramsey had been the most kind. It was she who had found a white ballgown belonging to Stephen's own mother and had taken in the waist and shortened the hem to fit Mary. It was she who had found a long scarf of white Brussels lace to use as a wedding veil, and it was she who had comforted Mary discreetly, directed the maid Bonny to help her, and found two other dresses for evening and day wear and fitted them to her.

Now it was Mary's wedding day, and she stood in a

warm daze, her cheeks flushed with fever, her eyes glittering and unseeing, as she was made ready. The wedding would be in the chapel at eleven. The vicar had come yesterday to rehearse them.

There was a knock at the door and Bonny went to answer it. A young footman stood there, a blue velvet case in his hands.

"From my lord to his lady," he said ceremoniously, but his eyes were lively and curious as he stared across at Mary in her white satin and lace gown. The skirts billowed about her as she turned from the full-length mirror.

Bonny curtsied nervously as she presented the blue case to Mary. Mary opened it awkwardly, then stared down in surprise at the contents. On the white velvet and silk lining lay a beautiful strand of pinkish white pearls, a matching set of long pearl earrings, and a large pearl ring on a dainty white band.

"Ah—the Huntingdon pearls, my lady," said Mrs. Ramsey.

"I am not—my lady—yet," said Mary slowly, huskily. Her throat was raw from coughing during the night. She rubbed it automatically, still looking at the beautiful pearls. Did pearls really mean a tear shed for every one?

"You will be in two hours," said Mrs. Ramsey cheerfully. She bent to draw out the white lace carefully. "There, let me look at you, my lady."

As the housekeeper studied her critically, Mary turned and stared at herself in the mirror. The dreamy white fabric drifted about her. The low bodice framed her creamy throat and set off the curves of her round breasts. Her red hair was combed and brushed to shining beauty and dressed down and about her shoulders, rather than drawn up in its usual severe coils as befitted a governess.

Mrs. Ramsey fastened the pearls about her throat and set the earrings in her ears. Then Mary put the ring on her finger, finding it only a trifle large.

"I—can't—believe," she said, half to herself.

"It's like a fairy story," burst out the silent Bonny, her brown eyes shining. "Like Cinderella and her prince. You come here, and he falls in love with you at once, and—"

"Bonny, that will do," said Mrs. Ramsey, but gently.

"Yes, ma'am," said Bonny, more meekly.

Mary thought how unlike a fairy story it was. She had threatened to bring suit against the Huntingdon family, and Lord St. John, his honor threatened, had taken the course he felt he must. No wonder he hated her. She shivered a little, thinking what might happen to her. What had she done? Why had she agreed to this strange proposal? She had not really agreed; she had been pushed, she thought, frowning a little.

Mrs. Ramsey brought the long scarf of Brussels lace, and the housekeeper and maid carefully lifted it and set it on Mary's head. It floated about her for a moment before settling down on the shining red-gold curls, drifting about her bare white shoulders.

Mary felt lost behind the white lace, peering out at the world through a mist. What am I doing? she thought again, desolate, frightened. She must be feverish. She felt too weak to fight the forces which were carrying her forward relentlessly into this marriage. Where was her usual strong will? Her Scottish courage? Her pride?

Another knock on the door. She started nervously. When Bonny opened it, one of the older male guests came in. He had consented to give her away, and had made vague flattering remarks to Mary which she was sure he did not mean. He was doing it only to please Stephen Huntingdon.

He was wearing a blue velvet suit, elaborate sapphire jewels at his throat and on his hands. He stared at Mary, then smiled at her kindly. He was a middle-aged man, and his wife was fat, dumpy, and nervous.

"Ah, the beautiful bride. My dear, how very charming

you look. One can understand Stephen's impulsiveness!" He put out his arm, and she placed her hand on it timidly. He patted it gently, as though he understood how nervous she felt.

He escorted her down the stairs, with Bonny and Mrs. Ramsey trailing behind them. They went down and down and into the underground regions of the castle, to the chapel.

At the door of the chapel, she smelled the heavy scent of flowers in the chilled air. She shivered. It was becoming real. She had been moving and living in a dream—now it was real. She could see Lord St. John standing in front of the carved wood altar, the candles shining there and along the chairs where the guests sat. Beside the castle guests there were guests from the village, some two dozen people in all. Lady Helena sat in a place of honor in the front row.

Mary stared forward up the silk-lined aisle, and felt she could not move. I am insane! she thought wildly. What am I doing here? I cannot marry him! I don't even know him!

The organ music changed. She suddenly realized it had been playing all along. Now there was a sort of march and she felt the tall man beside her gently urging her forward. Her footsteps fell in automatically with his, and she moved along the silk down the aisle. Her small feet were shaky, her hands icy cold.

She heard the rustle as guests turned to stare, and caught a few murmurs of approval at her appearance in the radiant white gown, the white lace veil.

As she arrived at the altar, Stephen Huntingdon turned. He stared down at her as she moved to stand beside him. She thought he started, that his arm jerked as she accidentally brushed against him in her fright. She was shaking now, alternating between hot flashes and chills in the icy chapel. The flowers on the altar were white and crimson, with jade-green ropes of leaves and vines twining between the baskets. On the altar were golden candlesticks and altar vessels. Jade and gold and crimson—those were the colors of the Castle of St. John, she knew by now.

But she must listen to the words. The vicar was speaking, slowly, sonorously, looking at them from time to time. She could not think about what he was saying.

Lance Tarrant, Viscount Greville, was standing beside Lord St. John as his best man. He was handsomely attired in blue velvet. She glanced again at Stephen, saw he was wearing crimson velvet with gold; at his throat and wrists were the immense rubies he favored.

And she—she was masquerading as a lady, she thought, in a feverish dream. In white lace and satin, with pearls—one might think she was a lady, instead of a governess. Only two weeks ago she had sat up all night with the baby, tending his croupy coughs, so weary she could scarcely get up when he demanded her again. And in the morning, instead of resting, she had had to hear the eldest boy's lessons, watch the younger ones at their play in a chill wind, and help with the linen sorting, until by afternoon she had been in a complete daze of weakness.

She swayed. Stephen's hand shot out and took hers firmly. His warm fingers closed over her icy hand, and he held her securely, his own arm under hers. She was able to continue.

She whispered the responses, heard Stephen's firm, commanding voice ringing out his. Although she caught the words, they did not register. Finally Stephen was turning to her, the lace veil was thrown back, and his face was very close to hers. She looked into the sherry-brown eyes and thought, he is angry, and—something else—but she did not know what other emotion he was feeling.

He bent closer. She closed her eyes and swayed. He held her firmly, one arm about her slim waist, the other hand gripping her hand. His lips touched hers, warmly, slowly, pressing firmly. Then he stood upright again.

They went upstairs, back to the warmer dining room, where a grand dinner was laid out. She sat next to Stephen this time, at his right, the filmy skirts spreading out about her legs, the wine glass at her place filled again and again, as toasts were offered, and the dinner proceeded. Across from her, Lady Helena was gracious and excited, her thin face animated as she listened to Lance Tarrant ramble on and on, telling stories about people she would come to know and reminiscing about the old days.

"This is a real pleasure," he was saying. "Always liked old Stephen, thought he would marry Angela. But I like you, Mary. I hope you will be happy with old Stephen. He's a fine chap. And you are like Angela, beautiful, though not so beautiful as my Angela," he hastened to add, drinking from the champagne glass thirstily, his tone thickening. "She was so very beautiful—"

"Greville," said Stephen, smoothly, with a frown. "Don't talk of the old days; they are finished and forgotten. Now is the day to think of our future—Mary's and mine."

It was the first time Stephen had coupled their names. Mary had an odd feeling, like a sudden unexpected happiness. She was married, and to this strange man, this handsome, hard man with the deep scar on his left cheek. She knew now that he had gotten it in a naval battle when his ship had been overrun by pirates, and he had fought saber to saber and hand to hand with some fierce, half-naked savages.

But there was much she did not yet know about him; well, she would learn—and soon, she thought, with a feeling like panic.

Lance was still speaking, thickly. "Lovely girl, Mary. Beautiful and intelligent. Intelligent as my Angela. Two of a kind, though Mary has red hair. You pick them smartly, St. John! I must say. Lovely girls. Hope you will be very happy."

Stephen was growing angry, Mary knew, and his

sherry eyes glowered. She could see his hand on his knee, clenched.

Another guest stood to offer yet another toast, and she smiled and nodded wishing she could lie down. She was so dizzy and tired, she could scarcely see. She began to cough, but stifled it by taking another deep sip of champagne, which made her dizzier.

Finally the dinner was over, and they rose to move on to the drawing room. She knew there would be a reception line, more drinking, more laughter, more talking, more gossip and curious glances at her.

She turned wearily away for a moment while Stephen was speaking in a low tone to his stepmother. She took a step or two and then collapsed, lying like a broken flower on the crimson French rug, her mind blurred into nothingness.

She came to in a sensation of being lifted and carried along by a wave, no, it was a wind, no, it was a man's strong arms. She could feel a heart beating under her cheek. She stirred, moaned, tried to open her eyes.

"Lie still, Mary," said a deep, commanding voice. She sighed, and lay still. It was so much easier to obey than to fight.

She was carried upward and down a corridor. She heard the murmured voices, concerned, questioning. She thought she heard Mrs. Ramsey's voice.

She was laid down on softness. It was so good, so restful, she just kept her eyes closed and drifted off again.

Time blurred. She was only vaguely aware of cool hands bathing her hot body, of voices murmuring over her head, of a cool gown slipped over her, of warmth of covers, and gentleness in touches on her hot, aching head. She vaguely heard the wind rising, and the sea pounding on the cliffs, but they were soothing.

Time seemed to slip by, and she did not have to get up and run to someone's bidding. She could lie still and rest her aching body, and she never wanted to move again. She was hot and cold; she coughed, and someone gave her honey and medicine. A firm hand stroked her forehead, and said to someone, "Is she any better, Mrs. Ramsey?"

"Oh, sir, not yet. She was very ill, sir. We must have a care it doesn't touch her lungs."

Murmurs, voices going away. She could not open her eyes, she was so weary. She heard Bonny's thin, dry tones, Mrs. Ramsey's soothing murmur.

She heard, clearly, Bonny's voice saying, "It will be better if her lord doesn't come."

"Hush, girl! You don't know—" and the voices dropped again.

She was puzzled, and wanted to speak, but could not. Why, why was it better if her lord did not come? Why did Bonny say that?

Finally, she wakened one morning and opened her eyes. She lifted one hand slowly, forgetting where she was. She stared about in wonder, finding herself in a strange room. It was jade and crimson and gold, twice as large as the bedroom she had occupied before. She could see through an open door to a bathroom of gold and white. Another door was opened to a crimson and jade sitting room, with elaborate furnishings. She frowned, puzzled, then began to remember.

She was married to Lord St. John, lord of this castle. And Bonny had said it was better if the lord did not come. She lay thinking about that.

Then she began to notice the flowers. At her bedside was a jade vase filled with bright, pretty spring flowers, only lightly scented. On the dressing table was a crimson Chinese vase with a dragon in gold trying to climb over it, filled with white roses. She could see baskets of flowers in the elaborate sitting room.

Mrs. Ramsey entered quietly, and her black eyes lit up

at once. "You are awake, my lady!" she said with pleasure. She came over to the bed and put her hand firmly on Mary's forehead. "And the fever is gone. You are quite cool now!"

Presently Lord Stephen entered, his face unusually gentle and concerned. He came over to the bed, and gazed down at her gravely. "You are better now, my dear?"

"Yes. Have I—been ill—for long?" Her own weak voice, and the thinness of her white hand on the jade bedspread, surprised her.

"Almost a week. You quite frightened us. The doctor said you had been feverish for some time, and were quite exhausted. He recommended much nourishment of bland types, and bed rest for you for another week."

His big hand came out unexpectedly, and he smoothed her forehead, brushing back her red-gold hair. She stared up at him, her eyes very big and green in the white face. He smiled down at her kindly.

"Thank you—for the—flowers," she said, not knowing what to say when he stared at her like that.

"You are quite welcome. I'm glad you can notice them. You were raving for a time about flowers and blood and a funeral, I think you said." He smiled, but his sherry eyes were grave.

She shook her head. "I don't remember," she said simply.

"I will let you rest for now. The doctor will come again this afternoon." And he went away.

The doctor warned her to remain in bed until she felt quite strong again, but pronounced himself quite satisfied with her progress. He seemed a kindly older man, rushed with his village practice, but quite sensible and considerate.

Lady Helena came to visit her that evening, chattering

on and on until Stephen came in to cut short her stay. Mary had the impression that Lady Helena was lonely and liked to talk to someone.

That night, she thought she was feverish again. She wakened from a restless sleep to hear subdued, deep, growly voices and the sound of wagons. Why would wagons be on the cliffs? she thought.

She lay awake, frowning, and finally got up and went to the long French windows. She had discovered that her new suite of rooms adjoined those of her husband, and were in a wing of the huge castle opposite from that where her first bedroom had been. She still overlooked the gardens and the white cliffs.

She opened the heavy drapes and peered outside. The moon was only a slim sickle. She gazed dreamily into the gardens, not thinking too much, until voices startled her again. She leaned forward, trying unsuccessfully to see where they came from. She did hear men's voices, and the slight, subdued clatter of wagon wheels. The cobblestoned path outside led back to the stables, she knew. Perhaps it was early morning, and someone was delivering supplies from the village.

She left the windows after surveying the beauty of the gardens, only dimly revealed on that dark night. She brushed past a small table, remembered that it held a golden clock, and bent to peer at the face of it.

She stared. It was twenty minutes past three.

Why would someone deliver supplies at that time of the night?

She stood there pondering until she realized she was chilled and shivering. She slipped into bed again, adjusting the warm covers about her. Her gown was not the heavy, practical, woolen one she usually wore, but a slim satin gown of palest cream and lace. She shivered until she finally warmed, and was soon asleep again.

In the morning, she remembered what she had heard, and thought about it; but she was unable to figure out what had actually happened. She suspected that it might have been a recurrence of the fever, but deep down, she knew it was not.

CHAPTER FOUR

MARY YAWNED and stretched in the wide bed. She was feeling so much more lively that she began to think impatiently of getting up and exploring the huge castle. After all, it was her new domain.

She smiled to herself, recalling how Bonny curtsied and called her "my lady," and Mrs. Ramsey brought the menus to her and consulted her about new curtains and refurnishing a guest suite.

The door opened quietly, and Lord Stephen peered in. Seeing her eyes wide open, he smiled and entered, shutting the door after him. He had not knocked as he came in from his suite of rooms.

For some reason, that bothered her today. It had not bothered her while she was ill; it had seemed a minor point during her fever and weakness. But now she was well again, she thought, and this was her bedroom, and he had no right—

But he was her husband. They were married. She lay quite still as he approached the bed, and gazed up at him as he came to stand over her. He held a large bouquet of white and red roses. He bent over her, placed the roses beside her, and touched her forehead with his hand.

"No fever at all for the past four days," he said with satisfaction. "I think you might get up for a time this afternoon, my dear. How would you like to come down to one of the living rooms and have tea?"

"Oh, I should like that immensely! I've been thinking how boring it is to lie in bed continually! I should not like being an invalid." She had the feeling she was chattering. The way he was gazing down at her disturbed her.

He was looking at her face, at her throat revealed by the low-cut pale green gown. Mrs. Ramsey had been quite clever at fitting and altering some of the gowns of Stephen's late mother, and Mary now had quite a wardrobe of nightgowns and negligees, as well as several dresses much grander than any she had ever worn. Mrs. Ramsey had brushed her long red curly hair this morning until it was shining and springing with life, and it hung clear to her waist. Mary lifted the sheet and blanket uneasily and drew it up to her bare throat. She felt warm and flushed, and wondered if the fever might perhaps be returning.

"What is your mother's family name?" asked Stephen abruptly.

Mary's green eyes opened wide in surprise. "Oh—she was a Bruce," she said proudly. "My father was a MacGregor, of course. The families disapproved, and my parents fled to England. But we are Scottish!"

He smiled down at her as though her pride and flashing eyes pleased him. "Somehow I had surmised that," he said gravely. "A Bruce and a MacGregor. Quite a combination. No wonder you have a will of your own!"

She lifted her chin. "Aye, that I have," she said, proudly.

"Good. I like a woman of spirit. But that is not what I came to inform you. I expect Christopher and Georgiana to return today or tomorrow. What rooms do you wish them to have?"

She jerked upright. He was now avoiding her eyes. This was his polite way of telling her, warning her.

"Oh—what rooms did—he—have before?"

"He had a suite of rooms next to his mother's. I believe he liked them. Mrs. Ramsey could inform you whether that suite plus the rooms on the other side of his would do for him and his new lady." There was a heavy pause.

"I will ask her," said Mary colorlessly.

"Good." He moved away from the bed, seeming relieved. She realized then that that was what he had come to tell her, that he had come to break the news to her that Christopher was returning. He probably thought she still loved him.

She lay pondering the situation after he had left. What *did* she feel toward Christopher? Anger, surely. Rage. Hurt pride. A desire for revenge. For a way of hurting him—perhaps.

Yet Stephen, of a higher social position than his younger half brother, was now her husband, and he was doing everything possible to soothe her hurt pride. As soon as Mary had recovered enough from her illness to begin making decisions, he deferred to her in household matters, and had seen to it that she was consulted even concerning his stepmother's wishes.

When Mrs. Ramsey entered a while later, Mary consulted her about the rooms for Christopher and his wife with cool command of herself. Mrs. Ramsey promised to make everything ready. Mary had a strong feeling that the process was already underway, that her own approval had been a mere formality. Yet Mrs. Ramsey was ever courteous, and seemed to value Mary's counsel and approval.

Bonny came presently and helped Mary dress. Mrs. Ramsey had laid out a lovely green silk dress with a matching velvet jacket to guard against any possible chill. Mary reflected how well she looked in it, though she was still pale. Her long red hair was tied back with a green velvet ribbon, so that it hung in a long, loose, curly mass down to her waist, informal yet attractive, and not wearing on her heavy, still-aching head.

Mrs. Ramsey helped her down the stairs. A footman was waiting to direct her and hovered over her until she was settled on a couch in the green drawing room. This was a larger, more formal sitting room, with jade curtains, jade silk-covered chairs and sofas, and many lavishly carved pieces of jade set about on the small marble-topped tables.

She settled into the cushions with a little sigh of relief. She was weaker than she had thought. It felt good to put her feet up and be covered with a robe, and sink back in the cushions. An unusually charming Stephen soon came in to sit with her.

Presently another man joined them. Mary had stiffened, thinking it was Christopher coming, but it was someone she had never seen.

"My dear, let me present to you the man who runs this estate, Evan Basset," said Stephen. "Evan, this is Mary Margaret, the new Lady Mary."

He made the introductions charmingly. Mary felt a sense of unreality as she held out her hand to the graying man. He smiled down at her with a quick kindness, as though he sensed her unease in the new position. He touched her hand with his lips. He was about six feet tall, slim, well-dressed in a brown velvet jacket and fawn trousers. On one hand was a well-cut carnelian ring with a crest in it.

"My dear Lady Mary. May I say welcome? My one regret in this whole glorious affair is that I was absent and unable to attend the festivities. Stephen has needed a wife, a lady, and you fit the position—beautifully."

"Thank you—so much," she said softly, in relief, and smiled up at him. She had heard about him from Mrs. Ramsey, and was a bit afraid of him, he had sounded like such a paragon. Mrs. Ramsey was always saying that Mr. Basset would know about this, that they could consult him about that, that Mr. Basset would have his own opinions on how to manage the other. But she found him to be generous and tactful. "I shall be requiring your advice frequently, I imagine."

He nodded his head as though in answer to some inner thought and gazed quietly into her eyes. "Whatever I can do for you—all you need is to request it, my Lady Mary. I have served the Huntingdons—I hope faithfully—for many years, and my services are yours entirely."

Stephen put his hand on the older man's shoulder affectionately, and the other looked at him with a little quirk of his eyebrows. They seemed very friendly with each other, and Stephen seemed more relaxed with him than with Lady Helena.

"My father, the late Lord St. John, was an invalid the last ten years of his life, Mary," Stephen told her. "If it had not been for Evan Basset's managing the estate while I was in the service, things would have gone poorly for us, I fear."

"Pooh, nonsense," said Evan Basset briskly, but he seemed quite pleased, a little flush on his tanned face. "You would have left the service and come home and managed wonderfully, I am sure of it. But of course your service in his Majesty's Navy helped us defeat Boney—" And they were off on discussions of the late war and Napoleon's escape and recapture after the one hundred days.

The conversation became military and technical, and Mary was content to lie back and let the men carry it. But suddenly, in came an influx of people, and she felt self-conscious once more.

For it was Christopher entering, with a plain, rather plump girl, and a radiant Lady Helena in a shining blue dress which overwhelmed the plaid dress and plain jacket of the dark-haired girl.

"Here is our new Lady Mary," cried Lady Helena. "How good to have you on your feet again, dearest!" she added, ignoring the fact that Mary was lying down. Her flights of language quite overwhelmed reality, Mary often had thought in their conversations. "Mary, dear, may I introduce my son Christopher, Viscount Courtley, and his new lady, Georgiana Demerest—oh, dear, I must get used to saying Georgiana Huntingdon. Darlings, this is Stephen's new lady!"

Georgiana gave Mary a nervous smile, a mere twitch of her lips, and turned to her husband. Christopher was looking knowing, arch, amused. Mary stiffened anew as the young viscount bent over her hand and kissed her fingers a little longer than polite manners dictated. She pulled her hand away a bit sharply, and caught Stephen's eyes gazing at her thoughtfully, watching her face. Was she flushed? She felt warm.

"How do you do," she said colorlessly.

"But of course you had met Christopher before! You had come to attend his wedding, you said," Lady Helena chattered on.

Evan Basset was studying them all with a slight frown, as though little escaped his notice. Mary was more concerned with the way her husband gazed at her and then at Christopher. Was there ever such an awkward situation, she wondered impatiently.

Tea was brought, and Mary asked Georgiana to pour for her, which the girl did with some awkwardness. Lady Helena looked on approvingly, sometimes correcting the girl in a low tone which still carried. The mother-in-law had evidently taken on the task, perhaps of her own choosing, of grooming her new daughter.

The tea, the conversation, the unaccustomed room and company, all combined to weary Mary. Presently she excused herself to retire to her room. Stephen insisted on accompanying her, but she refused to allow herself to be carried. "Indeed no!" she said hastily. "I am quite well, and I'm sure I'm much heavier, with all that Mrs. Ramsey has been feeding me."

"I'll carry her up," said Christopher brashly, and laughed at the frowns he earned from Evan Basset and Stephen.

On the stairs, as Stephen supported Mary on his arm, he said coldly, "The young puppy," and looked down at her.

She said nothing, feeling any remark would be damning.

"Are you really weary, Mary," he asked, rather roughly, "or are the emotions of meeting Christopher too much for you?"

"I feel no emotions at all," she said quietly. "Not at present. And if I did, they would be no concern of yours!"

"Indeed! They are quite my concern. You seem to forget that you are my wife!" They had reached the upper hall. He did not let her go, but rather held her more tightly as they turned toward their own suite of rooms.

"A marriage of convenience," she said rashly, her quick Scottish temper rising. "Convenience for both of us. Let us leave it at that, shall we not?"

A flash of anger flaring in his face, Stephen opened the door to her room and led her inside. "You have been ill, and are weak, or we should quarrel over this," he said coldly, his eyes flashing. "Have a care what you say to me, Lady Mary! I do not brook opposition. Someday we shall talk this out and come to some conclusions. Tonight —you had best rest." And he left her.

She was surprised to find she was trembling.

He was quite accurate in saying he did not brook opposition, Mary soon discovered, as she recovered enough to come downstairs more often the following week. He gave orders and expected them to be obeyed instantly.

Christopher alone would disobey him with impunity. At one order, the young man laughed and said pertly, "You are not on your quarterdeck now, Stephen! Will you throw me overboard if I wait till tomorrow to visit the farm? I had planned to show Georgiana my horses today!"

For a moment, Mary thought Stephen would rage at him; then the stern frown relaxed, the scar lightened, and he smiled. "Very well, then, young puppy. But see to it that you go tomorrow. I want that farm inspected and a report on it by the end of the week."

Mary overheard Stephen berating a groom for mistreating a horse, and was stunned at his language and his precise description of exactly what he meant to do to the man if he ever repeated such action. Another time, he bawled out the sedate butler for a dereliction and had the severe man shaking. She intervened at that point, for she knew more than Stephen about the situation.

"Indeed, my lord, it was not Wenrick's fault," she said quietly. "I myself heard him give directions about the wine. The groom brought the wrong bottles and chilled them. They had to be used then."

Stephen turned on her, and Wenrick's eyes opened wide, showing his surprise at her intervention. "Do not interfere, Mary!" said Stephen angrily. "It is his duty to see that all goes well. The wine was inferior!"

"Then after this, I shall help see to it that the proper one is brought," said Mary, facing him fearlessly, her scowl a match for his. "Let me inspect the cellars and plan the wine menus as well as the food. You may trust my judgment in this, for the Evertons were most particular, and spent much on their wine list!"

For a moment, she was afraid that he would "throw her overboard," as Christopher teasingly put it. But his scowl relaxed; he nodded reluctantly and finally agreed. For this purpose, she accompanied the butler to the cellars the next morning to take inventory.

Wenrick seemed uneasy about the matter. She did not know why until they entered the cellars and she looked about.

Cask after cask of brandy lay on the stone floors. On the walls were row after row of wine racks, full of bottles of white wine, rosé, red, port, sherry, burgundy, claret, sauterne, the finest French wines and brandies to be obtained.

They must have been smuggled in, she thought, though she said nothing. The butler relaxed a little, as she spoke calmly about the merits of one wine versus another to accompany various dishes.

She noted the dates on the bottles. Some had been purchased during the time of Napoleon. Others were much older, and must have been in the collection of the late lord. But the bulk of the inventory consisted of items purchased recently.

About the only way such bottles could have been acquired in such quantity, and with such labels, was through the smugglers! She had noticed subconsciously the quality and quantity of brandy and French wines on the dinner table and had thought little of it. Now she began to know, and to feel contempt for Stephen.

He had been fighting Napoleon's forces at sea—but at home he had allowed smugglers to sell him all this stuff. And this had helped finance Napoleon in his wild ventures, which had brought such grief to English and Scottish families. She thought of the men who had returned without legs, without arms, crippled in heads and bodies, their spirits crushed from imprisonment. She thought of the men who had not returned at all, of the families which had suffered for lack of husbands and sons and fathers—and she felt a fury which made her quite hot.

She returned to her own rooms to think. Stephen was a rake with a wild reputation in London. He had been a gambler and ladies' man, she knew from Helena's chatter and Christopher's jibes. She would not put it past him to indulge his taste for wines this way. Perhaps he thought he was justified.

At tea that afternoon, Mary was hard put to contain her feelings. Stephen himself brought up the subject of the wines, and asked her proudly what she thought of their collection.

"Indeed, my lord, it is the finest I have ever seen, though my experience is not vast," she said, keeping her eyes on the beautiful white porcelain teapot, decorated with red roses and green vines. She poured his tea carefully into the exquisite French cup and felt angry again. Her eyes were flashing as she raised them to his, and he lifted his cup at the same moment.

He stared down at her, and it was a moment before he put out his large brown hand and accepted the cup with puzzled eyes.

Evan Basset said placidly from his chair, as he balanced the lovely cup and saucer, "I think the late lord was an expert in this matter. Some of the wines he collected must be in such demand on the markets today that they would fetch a rare price! Your guests are honored, Stephen, when you bring out the wines, though some of them are not up to judging their merits!"

"All I know is when I like a wine or don't," said Christopher, and laughed about something to his bride. He was leaning over her chair, caressing the back of her neck with his hand; but he was looking at Mary as he did so. She kept her eyes away from his. He seemed sometimes to be filled with a strange anger, a crazy humor, as though he might regret his marriage.

Mary was finding a great deal to puzzle her and make her uneasy. She had formed the habit of riding alone for a time in the late morning on a mare which Stephen had carefully chosen from his stables for her. She and Betsy galloped off many an ill humor in those hours.

In the nearby village, she renewed acquaintance with Mr. Jones, the grocer. She enjoyed his dry humor and took his advice on where to purchase large supplies of foods for the castle. She also spoke to the innkeeper and came to know him and his kindness. She would never forget how he had gone out of his way to be gentle and considerate to her on her first strange day.

Sitting in the inn parlor for late morning tea, she sometimes overheard the other patrons, and as they became used to her sitting quietly alone, or talking sometimes to the innkeeper, they became more frank in their speech.

She caught talk of smuggling, terror, murder on the moors. She would keep her eyes demurely on her teacup, sitting thoughtfully, listening to the low, murmured conversation, hearing much, speaking little. And she became more and more troubled.

One morning a farmer from a village a dozen miles away was found dead near the cliffs. Mary went to the village deliberately the following day.

At the inn for her usual tea, she found the gossip running excitedly about the murder. She listened, then caught the attention of the innkeeper, who came over in his slow, deliberate way to speak to her.

"Who do they think did the murder, Mr. Ashwood?" she asked, as though casually interested. "Someone hereabouts?"

He spoke in a low, significant tone, gazing at her in a dark manner. "Smugglers, I fear, my Lady Mary," he murmured. "And there will be more trouble before there is less. It has gone on too long; it will end badly for us all. Is there no way to stop the smuggling?"

She gazed up at him, forgetting to pretend disinterest. "How should I know, sir?" she asked sharply. "You ask as though I might know an answer."

"Do ye not? Well, then, perhaps not. But ye be a smart lass," he said, thoughtfully, then colored. "I forget myself, my lady, forgive me. I do not mean to speak so. But ye be—like one of us, methinks, and understanding us. Not like those of the castle, with their noses up."

"I shall never forget your kindness to me when I arrived, Mr. Ashwood," she said, in her decided way, nodding her red head. "No, do not apologize for speaking frankly to me. I value honesty above all. Yes, above all," she added, half to herself, frowning down at her cup. She wondered for the hundredth time if Stephen were involved in the smuggling, actively involved now, not just buying French wines the way he had done before.

And if Stephen were involved in smuggling, did he know about the murder of the farmer? Indeed, did he participate in the smuggling? Did he, in fact, direct the smuggling? Stephen was a strong man, a leader. He was accustomed to commanding, to being obeyed.

The idea filled her with fresh dismay. For he was her husband, they had married, and he was her lord and master. Though he had done nothing about it yet, and it was still a marriage of convenience, sometimes she thought when he looked at her that her freedom would not last long. She was so mixed up, so confused, that she did not know what she wanted. She felt only that she could never love nor submit to a man who could be such a monster as to condone murder.

CHAPTER FIVE

AT DINNER that evening, the subject of the farmer's murder came up, and speculation ran wild. Evan Basset considered it a matter of some jealous husband.

"For all their quiet manners," he said, with a little laugh, "there is some flirting about among the women, especially the younger ones. I wager he had picked the wrong woman to try his hand on, and her husband found this way to be rid of the trouble."

The young bride, Georgiana, flushed. "Oh, surely not. I have lived in these parts all my life and—"

"And been highly sheltered by your parents," Christopher said, and patted her hand, agreeing with Evan. "No, if it had been smugglers, we should have heard about it by now. Rumors have a way of making their way to the castle, eh, Mother?"

"I pay little attention to those dirty matters," said Lady Helena, taking a thirsty drink of the French wine before her. "They seem all uncouth louts to me. One less is little matter."

Mary's eyes flashed toward those of her husband at the other end of the long, shining table. Across crystal and glass, across the elaborate silver epergne filled with white and red roses, their eyes met.

"I had hoped," he said, in his deep voice, moving a silver knife thoughtfully, "that with Napoleon's defeat the smuggling would end for lack of a market. But the excise taxes have not been wiped out, and men will forever smuggle the precious objects they can carry easily when there is a ready market and a high profit. I fear that this is part of the same pattern that often leads to murder and other crimes."

"Oh, Stephen!" cried Evan Basset, his face a little flushed. "Such folly! There is no smuggling around here. I would have heard of it, I assure you! We would be approached for a possible market, and I should give them short shrift."

"I know that, Evan. That is probably why we have not been approached," said Stephen. He was still gazing down the long table at Mary's face. She wondered what he read in it. "I deplore the smuggling, nevertheless, and fear it continues. There are markets inland, I feel sure, and perhaps as far away as London."

She gazed at him incredulously. How could he speak in such censorious, severe tones when his own cellar was full of the products of smuggling? She despised him for being a hypocrite.

She turned to the butler hovering near her. "Remove the course, and bring the sweets," she said, so curtly that Wenrick stared down at her in surprise.

In the jade drawing room after dinner, she dispensed coffee and tried to control her seething emotions. It was bad enough that Stephen was probably involved in the smuggling, at least was purchasing lavishly from the smugglers. But to deny it, to act so prudishly about it, was contemptible!

She excused herself early and retired to her room. After Bonny undressed her and was dismissed, she put on the pale green silk and lace gown and the matching lace negligee. She was not tired. Her brain raged on. She paced the floor, crossing to the windows and peering across the gardens to the sea. It was from there that they came, she thought. The sound of wagons she had heard at night was probably the smugglers making their regular delivery! And Stephen had raved on about how terrible their activities were!

Her door opened. She swung about and stood framed in the jade curtains of her bedroom windows as her husband entered. He was frowning. Bonny had left a branch of candles near the bed; it was the only light in the room. The flickering flames shone on her lace negligee, her long red hair, her small defiant face.

"I have meant to speak to you about the way you make free to enter my bedroom," she flung at him before he could speak. "I wish you would knock and ask my permission to enter!"

"Indeed," he said, and stepped closer until he was about three feet from her. She still stood by the windows. "You are very angry, I think. Why?"

She threw her head back, tossing it so that the red hair was blown about. He reached out, as though involuntarily, and caught a handful of the red mass in his hand. She flinched, stepping sideways, so his hand went to his side again. He stared down at her, his eyes narrowing.

"That talk of smuggling, that fine talk," she said, furiously. "When all the time your cellars are full of French wines and brandies."

"From my father's time," he said, slowly.

"With last year's date on the bottles? A likely tale!" And she stared proudly right into his eyes. "No, you are profiting by the smuggling! I can see it myself! And you can sit there with your family and guests and go on about how dreadful the smuggling is! Oh, yes, do not think to deceive me! I have eyes!"

There was a long, heavy silence between them. He did

not seem angry, just deep in contemplation. His eyes were studying her eyes and her face, wandering to her throat and gown, and back up to her face again. She felt taut as a bow, cornered against the windows, her fists clenched before her at her waist.

"I was in the navy most of the time these past years," he finally said, very quietly, with a tone which should have warned her. "Do you think I would condone the smuggling which profited Boney so much—and cost our lads in lives and us in limbs and eyes—do you think I would have fought as I did if—"

"You—fight!" she taunted him recklessly, her fists rising from her waist up to her heaving breasts. "You—fight! You probably did your fighting in the dockside inns and taverns—over the nearest wench! I can't picture you on the deck of a ship, with sword in hand! I have heard of your reputation with women! Those men I know who fought Boney would take no part in guinea smuggling or buying French wines—"

"You—dare to say—to me—" He took a step forward, another. He caught at her waist. She flinched and tried to wrest herself free. He pulled her to him, and she felt the heat of his body against hers. He put his head down toward hers, but she turned her head angrily away from his approaching face. He meant to punish her in the way which would humiliate her most, she thought, by forcing his kisses on her.

She was right. He caught at her thick red hair at the nape of her neck, and forced her head to turn back and up to his. His full, sensuous mouth came down.

She opened her mouth, baring her small white teeth.

"If you bite me, Mary, I shall beat you!" He muttered the words against her lips, then he took them with his own and drank deeply of the frightened breath she drew. His lips were hot, angry; the pressure of his arms crushed her against him. She was swept off her feet, her small slippers dangling as he lifted her up.

He carried her to the bed and dumped her. He followed her down, pressing her into the soft bedclothes. She tried to wrestle with him, to struggle and push him away. But she was as helpless as a small child in his grasp. His arms were stronger than iron bars, and his hand on her breast made her feel weak. He untied the lacy negligee, and his hand was on the silk of her nightgown.

She wriggled and cried out against him. "Let me go—bully, beast—let me go! I hate you—I tell you—I hate you!"

He did not listen. He was pressing her down, and his head was against her white throat. His lips wandered over her throat down to the white breast his hand was uncovering from the green lace.

She fought him, but it did no good. He was kissing her with a fierce passion that frightened her at first. His hands were moving over her possessively, learning her with a thoroughness she had never dreamed of. And to her shame, she felt herself weakening.

Then he moved more slowly, as he felt her yield. When she lay still and let him have his will, he grew more tender. She felt strange experiences, the pressing of his flesh on hers, the softness of his mouth as he caressed her, their nakedness in the bed. And she could not resist.

She felt weak, odd, incapable of fighting him any longer. Some strange feeling was invading her brain, her heart, her body. She did not want to fight. And when he took her limp white arms and put them about his neck, and lay on her, she more than yielded.

She could not restrain herself. She had never felt so hot, so carried out of herself. Her small body moved; she sobbed, tossing her head restlessly about on the pillows. And ever he followed her, turning her, moving her, so that she did his will and was where he wanted her to be.

When he took her finally, she was crying out with pleasure, feeling the emotions sweep wildly through her, as the land and beach feel the irresistible pulse of the sea in its tides. He whispered to her, wild words, urging her to respond to him—and she did respond, she could not help it. Her whole body was shivering in one wild reaction to his embrace, and he laughed softly as he began to finish.

It was a long time before she recovered. She lay limp in his arms. He seemed to be sleeping beside her. She felt drowsy, languid.

Later, he roused again and embraced her. She was weak, sleepy, unable to resist at all. He took her, a long sweet embrace. Later they slept deeply.

Much later, when she wakened, he was gone from her bed. She reached out her hand timidly, and was shocked to find herself disappointed at his leaving.

What had she done? She had meant to fight him. If he insisted on asserting his rights, she had planned to defy him, lie limply, never to yield her will or her body except when he forced her. He would pay dearly for anything he wanted from her, she had vowed.

She was furious when she began to realize what she had done. She hated herself for giving in so easily, no, more than giving in. She had responded with passion.

No wonder he had laughed!

In the morning, she took a long, hot bath, and eased the soreness of her limbs. Bonny dressed her in a white muslin trimmed with green ribbons—the color of her eyes, said the maid admiringly. She wanted to dress Mary's hair loosely, but Mary, her face flushed with color, insisted on having it braided and fastened severely on her head.

Stephen was late for breakfast, unusual for him. When he finally arrived, Mary was just finishing, the others well along. Christopher teased him.

"I haven't known you to sleep late, Stephen, except just

after you returned from voyages. What makes you so tired now?"

Stephen was unusually flushed, but he was composed. "Long hours of riding," he said, then his sherry-brown eyes flashed toward Mary's.

She felt herself blushing angrily. Was he teasing her, referring to their night together? How wicked of him if he was! She bent her head over the teacup. When Lady Helena left the table, Mary did also, murmuring some excuse.

She saw to some household duties, but her mind was not on them. She felt more and more angry. Stephen had conquered her so easily! He must feel very proud of himself, she thought bitterly. He and Christopher—two of a kind.

Lady Helena had been sneering at her lately, especially about the meals. They were not what she would have planned, she said, adding significantly that she would be happy to give advice about what ladies usually served. Georgiana had taken up her mother-in-law's tone, and went about with her nose in the air, making remarks about governesses who aspired above their station. They had not dared to make the remarks in Stephen's hearing, but they did not hesitate to do so in front of Christopher and Evan Basset. Christopher would usually chuckle, as though at a good joke. Evan Basset would look troubled and grave, but he said nothing. It was not his place to protect her, thought Mary rebelliously.

At lunch, Lady Helena criticized the wines. Mary had decided to serve a white wine with the lamb. "I always serve a red or a light rosé with lamb," said Lady Helena with a sigh. "Really, my dear, you must let me begin to advise you."

"It tastes quite good to me," said Stephen, coming out of some mild detachment of his own. He sipped the sauterne critically. "Yes, a dry white wine. Good."

Lady Helena pressed her lips together. "My dear Lord St. John, you spent so much of your life drinking the inferior stuff aboard ship, you cannot be considered an expert any longer." And she laughed a little, as though to let him know she was teasing. But her blue eyes were angry.

"Give Mary a chance. She will learn in time," urged Christopher pleasantly. He patted Georgiana's hand, but his gaze was on Mary's face and her white throat above the white muslin. "Anyone as pretty as Mary must be excused many things," he said. Stephen frowned at him, his lips tightening, then he glanced quickly down the table to Mary.

Trouble, always trouble, thought Mary to herself. They liked to sit and laugh and stir up trouble, these Huntingdons. They liked to laugh at her and tease her. Yet she was doing well; she consulted the wine books, Mrs. Ramsey, the grocer, and Wenrick, and did the best she could. But they did not appreciate her efforts.

And Stephen had laughed at her last night for yielding so weakly, the first time he had approached her. He must think her an easy mark. First, coming at Christopher's command when he sent for her, only to find him married and gone. Now, yielding to his embraces, letting herself be pushed about and harrassed by his stepmother and stepbrother, even Georgiana.

She pressed her lips tightly together. She wished she could think of some fine revenge—

She heard Evan Basset say something about smuggling, ". . . the guinea boats, which financed Napoleon; they smuggled the gold in guineas in the holds of ships . . ."

She listened no longer. She had an idea.

After lunch, she went to Stephen's study, tapped, and entered at his command. "You don't need to knock, Mary, my dear," he said pleasantly, rising when she came in.

She flushed, recalling how she had berated him last night for not knocking. The subject was a sore one. "I have only come to ask for some money," she said abruptly. He studied her face in some surprise.

"Why, my dear, of course. I have opened accounts for you in London. You may purchase whatever you wish. And you know you may buy whatever you please in the village. Any storekeeper will serve you—"

"I need some guineas, about ten guineas," she said, more quietly. Her small fists were clenched at her sides.

"Yes, of course." He opened the drawer at his side; it was crammed full of gold coins. He took out a handful and held it out to her. "Take whatever you wish," he said.

She shook her head. "Only ten guineas," she said persistently. To see that drawer full of coins made her feel a little ill. For ten guineas, she had come to Christopher. The money had meant nothing to him. It had meant everything to her. She had thought it meant that he loved her and wanted her and would protect her. Now, she knew the money had meant little or nothing at all, certainly not ten guineas, to the reckless young man who had thrown away a thousand guineas on a horse race recently.

She would not touch Stephen's hand as he held out the guineas to her. He finally laid the coins on his desk and said gently, "Take what you wish, then."

She counted out ten and picked them up. "Thank you," she said in a stifled tone, and turned to leave the room.

"Mary? I liked the wine this noon. I think you choose well," he said.

She did not turn back. He was only placating her, probably laughing at her behind her back. "Thank you, sir," she said, as properly as Mrs. Ramsey, and shut the door with a little bang of outrage as she left.

She arrived early for tea in the blue drawing room. The maid wheeled in the silver tray and set the cups out. Mary waited for the others to come, her hands clenched in her lap. She had a little silk purse with her today, one of Stephen's mother's. Everything she had, she thought, was from someone else. She was feeling sorry for herself as she waited, but her heart was full of rage and determination.

Georgiana came in, saw her, hesitated, then took a chair near the windows, as though determined to have little to do with her. Mary's mouth set. She did not offer tea, which she knew would be curtly refused until Christopher arrived.

Finally Lady Helena arrived, followed by Christopher, and then Evan Basset. Stephen was last, rushing in and apologizing. He looked weary and was still fastening his velvet coat. She remembered that he was going out to one of the farms that afternoon.

She poured tea silently, and the maid handed the cups around. She waited until everyone was served and the chattering became general and more easy.

She opened the silk purse and held the guineas in her hand. "Christopher," she said clearly, loudly. He turned to her at once. She held out the coins, and he accepted them automatically, and looked at them in his hand. "I must apologize for not returning your money to you earlier," she said.

He flushed hotly and tried to hand the coins back to her as though they were too warm to touch. "You owe me nothing, Mary," he said. Stephen stood up from his big chair and took a step toward them.

"You forget. You sent me ten guineas to come to you and marry you," she said quite clearly, her voice strong in her fury. She gazed directly at Christopher, ignoring the others, who had fallen silent.

"I did not," he said uneasily, turning from her, laughing a little. "Have you run mad?"

She took out the letter, deliberately, and unfolded it. Georgiana had gone white, then red. Lady Helena was uttering little nonsense words, "My, my, tut, tut, what is this, what is going on—"

"You forget very quickly, Christopher," said Mary, in a

chilled tone. "You met me at Evertons. You asked me to marry you. After you returned to Cornwall, you wrote to me and sent me ten guineas to come to you. When I arrived, I found you married and on your marriage journey. But let me remind you—I will read your letter aloud—" And she picked up the letter and began to read the passages about taking the stages—he would meet her—they would be married—

Christopher began to laugh. "Stop, Mary. Stop! You are embarrassing my wife! This is over and done with—"

Stephen said roughly, "Stop it, Mary. I won't have you reading that—"

Georgiana began to cry and ran from the room. Lady Helena stood up, muttering, "My, my, my," in an agitated way, and paced about. Evan Basset left the room after a long, thoughtful look at Mary, then at Stephen.

Mary folded the letter and put it back in the purse. Now that she had her revenge, she felt a little sick. She had hurt Georgiana, not Christopher, who was scarcely dented. Emotions rolled off his back quite easily, she thought. He was already laughing, and shrugging his shoulders.

"What a silly thing to do, to take me at my word and come here," he said, carelessly. "Nevertheless, I am flattered that you loved me so much that you came to me. I shall always remember that, dear Mary!" And he had the gall to reach out for her hand.

She snatched it from him, glaring at him like an angry cat. It was Stephen who spoke. "That will do, Christopher," he said in an icily controlled tone. "She is my wife now."

"All in the family," said Christopher, and sank down into his chair, picking up his teacup. His willful brown eyes were sparkling with malice as he gazed at her over the edge of the cup. "All in the family, dear brother!"

Mary drank the rest of her tea, not caring that it was cold. Later, she worked furiously with Mrs. Ramsey, planning the remodeling of rooms, overseeing some linen sewing, deciding menus for the next week. She did not want to be alone with her thoughts.

At dinner, Christopher was unusually merry, cracking jokes and ignoring the red-rimmed eyes of his wife. Lady Helena was almost silent, scarcely speaking to anyone, not saying a word to Mary at all. Georgiana sniffed into a handkerchief. Stephen was visibly annoyed. He scowled at his dinner and spoke harshly to any butler or footman who dared approach him. Only Evan Basset seemed his normal self, speaking placidly of nonessential events in the running of the estate. Mary was grateful for his calm. She herself was feeling bitterly ashamed.

After dinner, she escaped to Mrs. Ramsey's rooms as soon as the coffee was poured. The good woman seemed to understand her unease, and filled in the silences with practical advice about turning sheets and ordering more supplies from London.

Finally Mary returned to her room, where Bonny waited patiently for her. She let the girl dress her in a cream silk and lace gown and negligee, then Bonny left her.

She blew out the candles, removed the negligee, and slid into bed. She settled down gratefully. She thought she might cry a little and ease her sore heart. She had bungled badly, letting her Scottish temper guide her, instead of her common sense, and she had hurt the wrong people.

The door opened and then closed again. Stephen was coming toward her bed. He slid out of his robe, and before she could open her mouth to say a word, he was getting into bed with her. He said roughly, "My Lady Mischief!" and took her into his arms. "You have done nothing but cause trouble since—"

His own words were stifled as he pressed his mouth to hers.

CHAPTER SIX

THE FOLLOWING DAY, Mrs. Ramsey came to Mary with an air of great excitement. The carriage had come from London, she said, and there were packages for her. Should they be placed in her rooms, and would she like help in unpacking them?

In some wonder, Mary agreed. "But I have ordered nothing," she protested. "Perhaps they are for Lady Helena."

"No, my lady, no! They are for you," and Mrs. Ramsey bustled upstairs, her satin skirts rustling in her haste. Mary followed her and found herself half-running down the corridor to catch up.

In the jade and crimson suite, there were indeed a great many bundles and packages. Bonny was hovering over them, pink in her sallow cheeks, scarcely daring to touch anything without permission.

"Dear me," said Mary, in wonder. "What is this?"

"Your new clothes!" cried Bonny. "The clothes your lord ordered for you from London!"

"I declare, Bonny," said Mrs. Ramsey, exasperated. "You would tell a solemn church secret! There now, it's out.

Lord Stephen ordered many clothes for you, my lady, and here they are. I do hope they fit, oh, I do hope the colors are right! He took such pains to choose just the right ones for your coloring."

Mary blinked, told Bonny feebly she could begin to unpack, and watched in growing wonder as the contents were revealed. She began to feel quite excited, and happy, and ashamed of herself for her thoughts when she saw the contents. Stephen had indeed taken great trouble to purchase clothes for her. And he had thought carefully of what would please her.

There were white muslin dresses, just her size, with blue ribbons, and pink ribbons, and yellow ribbons, and green ribbons. There were bonnets of straw and felt and lace and velvet, of greens like jade and emeralds, of yellows like lemons, and cream chip straw. There were ball dresses —one of sheer yellow fabric trimmed with the finest lace, another of brilliant emerald green satin, another of dark green velvet soft as kitten's fur, and yet another of silver and white trimmed with small sparkling beads that shone in the candlelight.

And there were plaids—the Bruce and MacGregor plaids. She exclaimed over them in delight, lifting them from their tissue nests. Just the perfect ones for her, of wool and of silk, in her very own tartans. The Bruce plaid had red and wide green strips and narrow gold and white bands. And there was a brooch of rosemary to wear with it.

The MacGregor plaid had wide red, green, and narrow white stripes. The badge in the brooch was of the pine tree. What trouble Stephen had gone to, thought Mary, wondering at her own delight and strong emotion. He had asked her so casually of her mother's clan, and then had planned this delightful surprise for her. Now, for the first time in her life, she could wear the lady's tartans of her clans, in fresh new dresses.

And there was more. Underclothing of the finest silk and linen and lace, in white and ecru and cream. Night rails and matching negligees in green and cream and white, with lace flowing from wide sleeves. Stockings, and a dozen pairs of shoes. Riding boots of the finest Hessian leather. A riding habit in emerald green and another in smart black. And dashing, plumed hats to match.

Bonny and Mrs. Ramsey did most of the unpacking. Mary was still lingering over the plaid dresses, touching them lovingly, regretting that she had ever hurt Stephen in any way. All the time, he had been planning this for her! He must like her a little, she thought—and then she remembered the nights in his arms and blushed hotly. Yes, he did like her—more than a little, or he would not act in that way.

She put on the Bruce silk plaid for that afternoon and wore it to tea. Stephen was coming from his study as she raced down the stairways. Impetuously, she dashed up to him and held out her arms to show herself, smiling radiantly up at him.

"Oh, Stephen, these clothes! All these dresses—and my plaids! Thank you so very, very much."

He caught her hands, swung them, smiling down at her, looking more relaxed and carefree than he had for a long time. When she saw his smile, and the way his eyes shone, she wondered how she could ever have thought him entirely severe and humorless. He bent over and touched her lips lightly with his.

"You become the dress mightily, my Mary," he said. "You are blossoming like—like a Scottish rose." He stammered over his own compliment, and the red touched his cheekbones. They remained staring at each other for a long moment. And then a footman came along the hall, and the strangely happy mood was shattered. They went to the drawing room for tea, a little more sedate.

But there was a happy bird singing in Mary's heart.

Lady Helena commented on her dress and seemed to unfreeze slightly. She rambled on to talk of current fashions and her last time in London, and tea was more pleasant that day. Stephen seemed more relaxed also, and spoke of taking Mary to London one day soon.

The next few days were busy ones for Mary. Stephen had decided to give a ball to introduce her to the local gentry. She went to consult with Evan Basset in the study he had near Stephen's. He had another in the wing of the castle where he had his own suite. However, Mary had been warned that the wing was his own private quarters, by decree of the late lord, and no one ventured there without an invitation. "For indeed, he must have privacy, his problems have been so great. The late lord said that Evan should have whatever he wanted in the way of his quarters, for his great goodness and helpfulness in caring for the estate," explained Mrs. Ramsey. "He has done all of the work for years, until my Lord Stephen returned from the wars."

Their conversation was pleasant and businesslike. Evan Basset seemed to have the facts of the village and surroundings at his fingertips, and advised her carefully on whom to invite and what events to plan. It was decided to have a lawn tea in the afternoon and a ball in the evening in the huge ballroom and adjoining rooms of the castle.

He was cool, but pleasant and understanding. Mary felt like confiding in him. "I have doubts about the wines, Mr. Basset," she said. "Ever since Lady Helena criticized my taste—"

"I will be happy to advise you any time," said Mr. Basset, smoothing back his graying hair. "But I think you need not concern yourself too much. Lady Helena was looking for something to criticize, if I may be permitted to say so. And she has conventional ideas about wines—white with fish, red with strong meats, and so on. As long as

Lord Stephen is satisfied, have no doubts, for he is more knowledgeable than she about wines. Now, as to the ball—may I suggest that a variety be served. Some of the young people like their champagne punch, with plenty of fruit. The older people are inclined to like pink or white champagne or brandies. Wenrick might appoint two footmen to take charge of the wines exclusively, while three others attend to the buffet foods."

They discussed matters quite amiably, and she felt comforted when she left his study. He seemed so certain all would go well.

And indeed it did. That evening Mary wore the new lemon yellow ball gown, with its rich, full skirts of darker golden yellow, and a set of yellow topazes. The tiara was set in the rich red curls, and the gold made her red hair shine and glow. Long earrings of topaz hung from her small ears. She wore a huge topaz ring on her right hand, and on her left the diamond and emeralds from her husband.

Stephen smiled with pleasure when he saw her. He wore his crimson velvet, trimmed with gold and jade. "You look beautiful, Mary," he said. "I shall be fortunate if I can claim you for a single dance tonight!"

"You're stunning, Mary, you have blossomed out since you came here," said Christopher behind him, coming up to stare at Mary. "She's an asset to the castle, isn't she, Stephen."

Stephen turned away abruptly. "Yes, of course," he said, more coldly.

"Thank you both," said Mary, but felt a little uneasy at the look in Christopher's eyes. He had been drinking some already, she thought, and the servants were whispering that he and his wife had been quarreling. He seemed in a reckless mood.

Lance Tarrant, Viscount Greville, had come to stay for a few days. Mary greeted him gladly. He was so pleasant when he was not feeling morbid. He was always complimentary, and she felt at her best when he praised her appearance. She had several dances with him.

Stephen led her out in the first dance. When he put his arm about her waist, she suddenly had an odd feeling—a stifled, excited, breathless feeling. Was she faint from working too hard? Or was it too warm in the ballroom?

He swirled her about in the dance then brought her to rest near Christopher, who promptly claimed her for the next dance. Georgiana, near them, looking sallow in the wrong shade of blue, sent Mary a sad look that made her feel exasperated with Christopher.

She was glad to be claimed by Lance Tarrant, who proceeded to tell her how beautiful Angela had been on a similar occasion, when Stephen had given a ball to introduce her to his people. She had worn a gown of beautiful silver-blue, said her brother, proudly, and everyone had eyes only for her.

"She must have been lovely," said Mary, and wondered why it was hard to say that now.

"She was the most beautiful woman in the world. Stephen was deeply in love with her," the brother sighed, looking mournful. "You know, the night she was found dead, she had been gone for many hours. We had all been looking for her. She had not been seen since teatime. We have no idea where she went. But her slippers were covered with sand."

Mary looked up at him, startled. "Sand?" she asked. All she could think of was the beach, the foot of the cliffs. But Angela had been discovered at the top of the cliffs, not the foot.

Lance claimed her again later, rather the worse for drink, rambling on about his sister. Evidently the ball had vividly reminded him of his loss. Mary listened to him for more clues, but he just kept repeating how beautiful Angela had been, how clever, how sweet, how beloved by everyone. Except by the person who murdered her, thought Mary.

Christopher seemed to have been drinking also, but his steps were steadier as he claimed a dance. At the end of the dance, he remarked, "It's quite close in here. I say, let's step out on the terrace and get some air, Mary. Would it be too cool for you?"

"No, the May air is quite pleasant," she said, glad enough for the opportunity to slip outside. At once, she realized her mistake, for in the darkness, Christopher slipped his arm about her waist.

"I say, Mary, you are beautiful," he said huskily, and tried to draw her around for a kiss. She pulled herself back, with effort, because he was much stronger than she.

"Let me go," she said in a low voice. Others were on the terrace, several feet away.

"Don't refuse me, Mary," he said into her ear. "I know how it is with old Stephen. He's a bit cold, isn't he? We could be friends again, Mary. Like old times. I could meet you in one of the rooms upstairs—no one would be the wiser—"

She did not stop to think. Her hand came up, in a burst of Scottish temper, and she slapped his face hard.

He let her go promptly, but he was laughing as she rushed past him into the ballroom. He followed her, his hand to his cheek. When she turned to glare at him, she saw that his cheek was bright red with the imprint of her palm. And as she whirled about, she saw Stephen gazing at them from across the room where he stood with the squire's wife.

Mary was furious. Christopher had insulted her and thought no more about it than that! What was the matter with him? Did he mean to make Georgiana jealous? Or was he trying to infuriate Stephen? Or did he just do it to amuse himself? Trying to arrange an affair with her! He was terrible.

Insulting, that was it, she thought, as someone else claimed her for a dance. He meant to insult her. He thought so little of her, the "little governess" he had pretended to love, had sent for, then dropped completely, that he could treat her like this. She had dared to call his play, to reveal his true nature in front of his wife, his mother, and his brother. This was his way of revenging himself, of insulting her. He meant to show everyone that she was cheap and easily had.

How dare he!

She was still furious the next day. She had arisen early, to avoid the guests, eaten alone in her room, then gone out for a ride on her favorite mare. Only a gallop would ease her temper.

She let the mare out as soon as they were out on the moors. She let her run freely, riding out her own temper until she felt more calm. Christopher meant to harm her, she thought. He would wreck her marriage if he could. All for malice.

And what about her? How did she feel about Stephen now? She thought of his roughness, his coldness at first, and the new tenderness rising between them. She thought of the way he kissed her in bed at night, the way he held her in his arms, his gentleness in making love until emotion overcame him and he was hard and passionate, but still sweet to her.

She felt hot and flushed when she thought of Stephen in bed with her. He made her feel emotions she had never dreamed of feeling. And at the ball, when he had put his arm about her waist and drawn her close, she had felt half-faint with some strange emotion. What was it? She had never felt like this before in her life. She drew the mare in and they walked along slowly, down by the moors to the edge of the forest near the farms.

Her eyes dreamed, her mouth quivered in a smile. Stephen, she thought. Stephen—Stephen. How strong he was, how obstinate, how difficult, then abruptly considerate. He was so used to commanding that he did not stop even in bed!

She lifted her head impatiently. Oh, she was insane! She really hated and despised Stephen. He had pretended to be a fine officer in His Majesty's Navy, fighting Napoleon. And all the time he was smuggling, or at least buying the profits of the smuggling. And he could lie and cheat and pretend to honest indignation—

She lifted the reins and urged Betsy on at a faster pace. Afterwards, she was not at all sure what had happened. She was entering the forest, and it was abruptly darker after the sunshine on the moors. All of a sudden, Betsy stumbled, and Mary, dreaming, was flung forward and over on her head.

It stunned her, and she lay in a daze. She was face down in thick pine needles, and she finally had sense enough to turn her face to the side to breathe. But all the wind seemed knocked out of her. There was a deep pain in her side and shoulder. She did not want to move.

"Hallo, there. Hallo," said a sullen deep voice. A shadow bent over her. She could not move, she blinked at muddy boots beside her. "Hallo—are ye hurt?"

"Yes," she managed to say, faintly.

The man knelt beside her, straightening her arms and legs with careful hands. But she still felt like screaming until he stopped. "Bruised only, betides," he muttered. She gazed at his scowling dark Cornish face. One of the local farmers, she thought.

"Well, Lady Mary, no help for it. I best carry you home to my missus," he said simply. "She will know what to do for you."

She nodded weakly. "My—mare?"

"No mare hereabouts. She be gone home, chances are."

Carefully he lifted her in his arms, settled her, and began to walk with her. She was in a daze of pain and shock. She closed her eyes. It seemed like a long walk. Then she heard voices, childish voices, a soft woman's voice. The man carried her into a cottage, where it was darker, and laid her down on a hard couch.

A woman bent over her, a small woman made thick with pregnancy, her face gentle. A boy of about ten and another of seven tugged at her skirts, and a small girl of three gazed solemnly from the foot of the couch.

The woman opened Mary's dress timidly and felt along the arm and shoulder. "Something pulled and swollen there, Jeremiah," she said in a musical voice. "Ye best send to the castle for a carriage for her. Ye can't carry her like this. Hurt her too much."

Jeremiah nodded and clumped out. The woman made Mary comfortable, smoothed ointment on the shoulder and arm and more on her hips and thigh, then gave her some tea.

Jeremiah returned, too soon. Anne questioned him sharply. Mary heard their whispers. "Mr. Jason, he be going up that way, he will give the alarm," said Jeremiah. "Damn them, they left a note on my stables again! Want it left unlocked again tonight."

"Oh—no, Jeremiah! Oh, no, no—" And Anne began to weep softly.

"Damn them, cuss them, I won't do what they say—damned lot of them!"

"But if ye don't do as they say, they will have you killed also!"

The words in the soft, musical tone, the heartbroken break in her voice, filled Mary with horror. She lay with her eyes closed, pretending to sleep, as they whispered about it. Jeremiah finally gave in to his wife's pleadings and said he would leave the stables unlocked.

Mary was deeply puzzled and alarmed, but dared not show it. They had not meant for her to overhear them. The small girl came and sat beside her and touched her forehead importantly. Mary opened her eyes and smiled at her, and the girl finally returned her smile.

Anne Shaw came back in, wiping her eyes. "Lucille, don't you bother my lady!" she said rather sharply.

The little girl said gently, "She be liking me, mum."

"Yes," whispered Mary. "I like—you—Lucille."

The girl smiled again, and patted her forehead soothingly.

Presently a carriage drove up. Mary thought the castle might have sent a groom for her, or even Wenrick. But Stephen himself strode in, bending his head at the low cottage door. His eyes went toward her at once, and he was at her side in a moment, his face concerned.

"Mary, what in hell happened to you? What the devil—are you badly hurt?" And he bent over her, touching her forehead and smoothing back her red hair.

"The mare—Betsy—fell with me—"

"Tripped over a wire strung in the path," said Jeremiah Shaw unexpectedly, his deep voice rumbling. The two men stared at each other.

"A wire—on the path—," said Stephen slowly, his face darkening.

"Meant for another body, belikes," said Shaw, sticking his hands behind him. There was a small silence in the room.

"I'll come back later. You'll show me the place," said Stephen crisply, and nodded to them. "Thank you for taking care of my lady. I am grateful to you."

He lifted Mary in his arms and carried her out to the carriage. He set her in, pulling the robes about her very tenderly. But she noticed that Anne Shaw shrank back from him and said little to him. The boys imitated their father and stuck their hands behind their backs to watch gravely as the two of them started off.

Only small Lucille smiled and waved back when Mary waved to them. Mary noted the expressions on their faces.

They had been nice enough to her, almost friendly. But Stephen—they were afraid of Stephen. It showed in their looks, their defiance, their sideways glances.

"Now tell me what happened, Mary," said Stephen.

She leaned her head back and closed her eyes. "I was riding—along the moors—," she began wearily. She told him what had happened, little enough. But she had bruises to show for her mishap.

Stephen carried her up to her rooms and sent for Mrs. Ramsey and Bonny. They bathed her in hot water to bring out the bruises and put her to bed, exclaiming over the injuries. She was glad enough to rest, drink a soothing tea mixture, and sleep. She felt shaken.

Later, she thought, she would think about what had been said. The door was to be unlocked to the stable. The wire had been strung across the path—meant for another body. Another murder might be committed—who, why, for what reason? She had to find out.

CHAPTER SEVEN

MARY HAD LITTLE opportunity to find out anything. She was confined to bed for two days, and to the castle for another week. She was quite badly bruised and shaken, and Stephen was stern and concerned about her.

She tried to question Bonny, but the village girl turned unusually sullen and quiet, plainly afraid to speak. Mary ceased her questioning when Bonny turned from her and hung her head.

Stephen came in often. He would seat himself on the bed and talk to her. He had discussed the incident with her after going back and looking at the wire strung between two trees. He said he did not understand for whom the trap had been laid. But no one could have known Mary was coming along that way.

Mary thought not, too. She had seen and heard no one. However, she had been dreaming, her thoughts and mind far away. She had been thinking about Stephen, and his lovemaking, and his sweetness to her in bed. She did not admit that to him, only that she had been riding without concentrating on her surroundings.

"You must not ride alone again," he had told her firmly.

"If I am not here to go with you, take one of the older grooms."

She came to look forward eagerly to his visits, as she was confined to bed or to the couch in the jade sitting room. He would come in from riding on the estate, sit down beside her, and speak eagerly about matters of concern close to his heart.

She began to feel more like his wife. He was confiding in her. He would tell her about the tenants, the problems on a farm, the squire and his suggestions, or the vicar and what he had said. There were always more problems, it seemed, and they were coming to him with the problems, as they had come to his father years before.

Once Stephen ran his hand through his thick dark hair, rubbed his face and confessed, "It was easier to run a ship than this place, Mary. This gets complex. On deck, I'd give an order, or settle a matter, and that was that. Now I have to consider how the vicar will feel about it, or what Mrs. So-and-so will say, or whether an old biddy will object to this, or how it has been done for centuries. God!"

She gave a soft laugh, leaning back in the cushions, surveying his irritation with some amusement. "So the world isn't the way you would order it, Stephen? Too bad! Perhaps in a year or two you will have all as neat and orderly as your quarterdeck!"

He gave her a look of fury, tempered with rising amusement. "My Lady Mischief," he said, unexpectedly, and leaned forward to press a warm kiss on her nearest cheek. "You would defy me on that quarterdeck, I'll warrant! I wouldn't have you as a midshipman! You would be confined for discipline three-quarters of the time!"

She chuckled again, knowing her cheeks were flushed at his action and words, and the look he gave her. "Oh, I'm not so easily ordered about as your midshipmen, sir!"

He made a grimace and took her hand in his. "No, you

are not, Mary. Perhaps that is why I am pleased I chose you as my wife. It will be enjoyable to tame you!"

"Tame me!" She sat up straight, indignantly, to find he was watching her with a teasing, intent look. "You cannot hope to do that, sir! I am a MacGregor!"

"You are a Huntingdon," he corrected her softly, dangerously smooth in tone. "And you will come to hand in time, I warrant! But I was telling you about the Shaws. I think Mrs. Shaw is close to her time. Would you like to ride over there tomorrow, if you feel well enough?"

So definitely he changed the subject, but she did not forget what he had said. Tame her, indeed! He would find he had a handful, a task beyond his by no means small powers!

Stephen began taking her out in the carriage on tasks about the estate. As they went, he explained to her some of the problems. She found them more than fascinating; they were all consuming. She went again and again to his study on their return, to trace their journey, locate the farms they had visited, sometimes to ask him again for details of the farmland and its treatment or the people who lived there. He was always eager to tell her of them, and the warmth of his tone spoke of his interest in the matter.

They spent long hours discussing future plans on the estate. He had returned from the wars to find some of the farms in poor condition, for Evan Basset, he remarked, had more than enough on his hands with running the castle, the forest lands, some of the farms. It would take the two of them full-time to manage all.

Mary often had it on the tip of her tongue to say that if his brother Christopher were more help to him, it would be easier all around. But she found it difficult to speak of Christopher to Stephen. After all, she had come here to marry the one man, and had married the other. Stephen still watched her reactions sharply whenever Christopher entered the room, whenever they spoke to each other, when Christopher teased her or ignored his wife to pay attention to Mary.

Mary, in turn, was still furious with Christopher for his insulting suggestion. She took care never to be alone with him.

A few days later, she and Stephen were visiting near the Shaw cottage when a small Shaw boy came running to their carriage.

"The doctor—the doctor—," he panted, his eyes wide with fright. "Mum is paining hard."

Stephen took him up in the carriage, and they rode back to the Shaw place. They found Jeremiah bending over his wife, who was in labor, crying out in a way that made the children weep in fright and sympathy.

"If you will go for the doctor, I'll stay here with Anne Shaw," said Mary, briskly, beginning to set about the kitchen. "The babe is determined to come, I'll warrant. Little Jerry, take your brother and sister outdoors, and don't wander far. Your mother will do fine once the babe has come."

Stephen hesitated to leave her, his face troubled. "Do you know what to do, Mary?" he asked, his gaze flinching from the twisted face of the pregnant woman, writhing on the couch. "She is in such pain—"

"Aye, I've helped Mrs. Everton through six births, and other women there. One of the doctors said I should have been a nurse," she said proudly, rolling up her sleeves. "Now, Mr. Shaw, if you will fetch some cloths—"

Stephen went on his way, and Mary busied herself with the woman. The baby was beginning to come, but he was coming breech first. Mary set her mouth. It would be difficult.

She had seen only one such birth, and heard the women murmur their forebodings. But a clever, patient doctor had helped the woman, and the baby had come right. She spoke to the rigid, pain-wracked woman.

"Anne, I'm going to try to turn the babe before he comes through. Will you trust me to help you?"

"Oh—yes—Lady—Mary—yes—," gasped Anne. She was twisting. "What is—the matter?"

"He's trying to come out wrong end first," said Mary, calmly. "So I'll turn the stubborn one around."

She worked carefully, as she had remembered the doctor doing, and to her relief and Anne's, it began to turn. Jeremiah Shaw watched helplessly, coming with fresh cloths and hot water, but unable to do much. Finally there was a pause, as Anne rested. Mary knelt beside the bed, watching, waiting.

Stephen drove up. She heard him coming in, heard the doctor's voice. "Now, now, no need to rush. I've delivered younguns afore—"

Mary frowned. She turned her head as the doctor stumbled in. She had met him twice and had not been impressed. Now she saw that his face was red and flushed, his feet unsteady. Worse, there was a strong odor of liquor about him.

She stared at him in distaste as he set down his bag and came to the bed. He had not paused to wash his hands, and they were muddy. Mary set her mouth.

"Best wash up, doctor," she said, crisply.

"It's clean dirt, I been farming," he said, and bent to the woman. Mary slapped his hands back.

"Ye'll not touch her in that condition!" she cried out, her Scottish temper flaring. "And what do ye mean, coming to help at a birthing in your disgraceful condition? Why are ye drinking this early in the day? Don't ye honor your profession?"

The doctor stared, grimacing, his face even redder.

Stephen was gazing gravely at them both, his face troubled. Jeremiah Shaw stood stiffly near the head of the bed. Anne's eyes were closed; she was nearly unconscious from the pain of the difficult birth.

"You don't speak to me like that, missy!" said the doctor rudely. "Evan Basset hired me, and he is my master! You'll have him to reckon with!"

Jeremiah Shaw stirred. "She don't mean nothing," he said, strangely, his tone pleading. "We be glad to have you help at the birthing, doctor—"

Mary blinked in amazement. "Help at this birthing? That he will not!" she said, enraged. "The baby is coming wrong. He needs good help, not the help of a drunken sot!"

"I'm a doctor," said the man, and bent down again, his hands reaching out toward the tormented flesh.

Mary struck him away again, standing up this time and facing him. She put her fists on her hips and tossed back her red hair. "Ye are not fit to be a doctor!" she said clearly. "Stephen, I would that ye discharge him! I've heard tales of his doctoring, and *no* doctor is better than this one."

Stephen stirred and came forward. He said gravely, "Do you mean this, Mary? Can't he help even in this condition?"

"I mean it," she said bravely. "I can manage better without him. I'll bring the babe, and do it well. But not with this drunken disgrace here!"

"Then you are discharged, doctor," said Stephen quietly, with the cold, dangerous tone that made many people quail. "Come out of here. The fumes from your breath are stifling!"

The doctor tried to fight free of Stephen's grasp on his arm. He was so red his eyes bulged out. "You'll regret this!" he blustered. "Wait till Evan Basset hears about this! He hired me!"

"He is not master of St. John," said Stephen Huntingdon coldly. "I am lord here, if you need reminding." And he pulled the doctor away and out the door.

The doctor called back, "You'll regret this! You'll regret this! Wait till Evan Basset hears—"

Jeremiah Shaw spoke in the stillness as the doctor was dragged away. "This be a mistake, my lady. I know ye mean well, but my Anne—and the whole village—oh, dear God on high, what will be happening?"

Mary looked at the sturdy farmer in great surprise. "Do you believe his threats? What can he do? My Lord Stephen is master here, you know that!"

He gave her a strange, haunted look, but Anne cried out, a great, convulsive cry. Mary whirled to the bed and bent over her. She soothed her, gave her a pillow to clutch, and helped the babe as it made its determined way out of the writhing body. It came head first, she was relieved to find, and it came smoothly. In a few minutes she held the squalling red body in her hands.

She gave the baby to Jeremiah, who seemed to know just how to handle the child. Mary gave all her attention to taking care of the afterbirth and making Anne comfortable. After a few sips of tea, and a look at her baby, Anne fell into an exhausted sleep.

Mary bathed and oiled the baby. She heard voices outside, and presently Stephen came in. With him were two ladies, and Mary was relieved to see that they were the squire's wife and another woman from the village.

Mrs. Demerest was a sensible, plump woman, much like her daughter Georgiana in coloring, but with more poise and sense. She said crisply, "I heard in the village that Anne Shaw was laboring, so we came to help. It looks like Lady Mary has everything in hand." And she gave a solemn, approving look at the sleeping mother, and the plump babe being wrapped in blankets.

Mary gave her a weary smile. "He came fine, Mrs.

Demerest, but he started out breech, which is trouble, as you would well know. I turned him, and out he came like a fine boy."

Mrs. Demerest was surprised. The village woman nodded in great amazement. "Not many as know that," said the woman. "Let me take the babe, Lady Mary. You look like you are weary." And the two women took over with sensibility and calm.

Mary was able to leave with Stephen then, and in the carriage she leaned back with a great sigh of relief. "Thank you for discharging that no-good piece of nothing of a doctor," she said at once.

Stephen chuckled. "I thought you had discharged him, Mary," he said, giving her a mischievous look. "You are the master of St. John now, I'll warrant."

She dared to cuff his arm affectionately, and he responded by putting it about her in a great hug. "Oh, you will ever tease," she said, comfortably. "Aye, I am weary! I could sleep a week after that. But the babe is beautiful, and Anne will not be bad off."

She was silent then on the long ride home, and her eyelids were drooping before they had arrived at the great gates of the Castle of St. John. She reached her own rooms and fell on the bed, to sleep for several hours.

She wakened in time for tea. Dressed in one of her favorite plaids, one of the Bruce tartan, she went downstairs. Lady Helena was there, and Georgiana, and both greeted her with greater friendliness and warmth than usual.

"I heard you were able to help with a difficult birth," said Georgiana, blushing at her own daring to speak. "Mum sent word by the footman that if it hadn't been for you, Anne's babe might have died, and she been badly torn. She said you showed great experience."

"Experience, aye," said Mary, taking the speech in stride, though it amazed her. She sat down at the tea table. "Your mother will not join us for dinner, I take it? She was very occupied with helping at the Shaws."

"No, she can't come this evening, and sends her apologies. You impressed her, Mary. She doesn't often speak so warmly of someone's nursing. I remember a time—" And she went on happily into a little story about the village. It was one of the few times she had spoken with any warmth and ease. Mary was glad to see the change in the girl, who was so often silent and uncomfortable, even in her husband's presence.

Evan Basset entered and went directly to Mary. "I must apologize for the doctor, Lady Mary. He was drunk, about which I have warned him. The scare was good for him, and I'll warrant he will not soon try this again."

She gave him a chilly smile. She could not forget the man's rudeness, his threats, and above all his dirt and poor condition of mind to attend a very sick woman. "That should not matter to us, Mr. Basset. He will not again attend anyone in this county! Stephen has discharged him."

"But you will intercede for him," said Mr. Basset, gravely, his gaze troubled. "He is a good doctor, well recommended—"

One of the maids helping with the tea dropped a plate of sandwiches. Mary did not turn, but Mr. Basset wheeled and stared at the girl. Mary frowned a little.

"I judge for myself, and the man is not capable of doing a decent job," she said crisply. "No, I do not intercede for him. I asked Stephen to fire him. He is to be gone as soon as possible. No doctor for a short time will be better than the damage a drunken sot can do. There are midwives about. We will find a better doctor as soon as we can."

"But the man has been here for a dozen years!" protested Evan Basset, his smooth cheeks flushing a little. "I beg you, Lady Mary—"

Stephen and Christopher entered the room and soon learned the cause of the argument. Georgiana was listening, troubled, her plump cheeks flushed, her eyes thoughtful.

Christopher gave his blunt opinion of the matter. "I would not trust that so-called doctor to handle the horse of an enemy racing against one of the best bloods in my stable! No, no, even an enemy would deserve better than him."

"Has he always been like this?" asked Stephen casually, reaching for the cup which Mary was handing him. His sherry-brown eyes met hers for a moment, and she realized he was not at all casual about this.

"No, no, of course not—"

"Yes, for years," said Christopher bluntly.

"Yes, he is always like this, just terrible, papa says," cried out Georgiana. "I'm glad he's going. He came to treat me one time, and I cried like a river and would not have him again, though I hurt so much!" Then she blushed vividly.

"Then he goes, and we will find another, more able doctor," said Stephen placidly, going to his favorite large chair and settling himself. He accepted a plate and sandwiches from the nervous maid who had dropped the plate before. "No more of the matter. Christopher, how did your horse race today?"

Christopher's face lit up. He went to sit with Stephen and enlarge on how well the horse had run, what hopes he had for it. Evan Basset sat silently with them, speaking little, his face dark for a time. Before he left, Mary was relieved to see him more placid. Perhaps the doctor was a good friend and Evan Basset hated to see him lose his position. She hoped Mr. Basset would not bear a grudge, for Stephen seemed to value his work highly.

Stephen came to Mary that night and made love to her.

He was very gentle at first, and she relaxed and began to enjoy it. She did like his lovemaking now, she finally admitted to herself.

He was kind in bed, so slow at first, and gradually building up her emotions and feelings. He talked to her sometimes, about casual matters, and was sweet to her, considerate of her reactions.

Now, as she lay in his arms, she began to think what it would be like to bear his child. The little baby in her arms that day had roused more motherly instincts. Would she like to have Stephen's baby?

Yes, she thought. A baby boy, like Stephen, with his dark curly hair and sherry-brown eyes, gazing up at her soberly, or with Stephen's quick, rare smile. She turned and pressed her face to Stephen's bare shoulder, and he was quick to note her response to him.

He whispered, "My Mary?" and drew her closer. He never said that he loved her, and she began to feel pangs about that.

If only he were not involved in the smuggling. If only she could be sure of him, and what he was really like. But she knew there was much more to Stephen than appeared on the surface. He knew quite well how Evan Basset would react to the discharge of the doctor, and he had handled it smoothly and rather innocently on the surface. But underneath—what must he have thought of Jeremiah Shaw's fear and distress over the firing of an obviously incapable doctor?

Anne had been too wretched to react to the doctor. But Jeremiah had been ready to let him touch the wife he obviously adored. Why? Mary thought and thought, and Stephen noted her absentmindedness.

"Mary—where are you?" he whispered, bending to her.

"Here," she said simply, and put her bare arms about his neck.

"Don't leave me, then," he said, and brushed his mouth against hers. "I won't let you leave me, even in thoughts! Kiss me."

And her mind swam and she forget everything in the world but him.

CHAPTER EIGHT

MARY WAS AMAZED at herself when Stephen went away for a few days to look at a distant property which had been neglected in recent years. She was conscious at once of dismay, or a depression of her spirits. Why?

She should be relieved, she told herself sternly. He was bossy, obstinate, willful, domineering, and she ought to be happy to be out from under his thumb for a few days. But she was not. She missed him terribly. She would stir during the night, reach out for him absently, and, finding him gone, would come wide awake and lie sleepless for a time.

During the day, she found herself going to his study with a problem, to tap on the door and hear no response. She would slip inside, walk over to his desk, perhaps sit in his huge chair for a few minutes, looking at the charts of the estate, thinking about him, missing him, wondering if he missed her.

Christopher was a nuisance. There seemed to be a devil in him some days. He raced his horses recklessly, for all his devotion to them. He was rude to his mother, to his wife, until Georgiana wept, then he was remorseful. He teased Mary unmercifully, watching her reactions with wicked, mischievous eyes.

And he had approached her again about an affair. She marveled at his crudeness, his daring. He had come to her in the gardens, in midmorning, as she was directing the gardeners about the late May plantings. After she had left them and was strolling through the rose gardens, studying them critically, he joined her.

He walked along with her casually. "You are like a Scottish rose, Mary, all prickly, but so beautiful and fragrant," he said, looking down at her devilishly. She flinched. Stephen had compared her to a Scottish rose. That was a private matter between them, she thought, and she wanted no other man saying such things to her.

"Thank you, I am sure, Christopher," she said, in such a chilly tone that he flung back his handsome head and laughed.

He turned coaxing, and tucked his hand in her arm though she tried to pull away. He bent closer to whisper to her, "Mary, Mary, you are teasing me! You don't love Stephen, you love me. He is gone now. Why don't you meet me in the upper hall—we can go to one of the bedrooms—"

She yanked herself away swiftly, turning on him in a rage. Her green eyes blazed. "Ye insult me again? How dare ye! I'll have no affair with you, ye scum! If Stephen knew—"

"But ye won't tell him, will ye?" he mocked her accent, and managed to squeeze her hand. "Ah, ye'll give in to me one day, my pretty Mary! Ye still love me, I know!"

She stared at him, her mouth tight. "I do not," she said flatly, "and I never did. Ye were the means I was using to rescue myself from an impossible work! That was all. I'd have married the devil himself—"

His eyes flickered as he stared down at her. "And you did, eh, Mary? Is that why you married Stephen? Because you were desperate enough to marry the devil himself? If you only knew Stephen, the real man, the bullying, hard man he is—"

She turned and left him, unwilling to hear his words. She raced back to the house, and threw herself into her duties almost desperately. She tried to erase from her mind that hard, honest tone Christopher had used at the last. He had meant it; he believed that Stephen was putting on an act, that he was really a hard devil—

Was he? She knew he could put on an act, she had watched him hiding his rage, smoothing his own temper to control others, hiding his feelings from Evan Basset to keep a situation cool. Yes, he could be a hard man. He wanted his own way, and he was determined to have it.

Christopher drank heavily at the noon meal. Lady Helena tried to tease him into giving up the glass, but he cursed her and his wife, and raced out of the room. In late afternoon, a footman came to Mary as she was preparing to serve tea in the jade drawing room.

"My lady, there is a farmer who would see you," he murmured, apologetically. "He insists it is urgent that he see you at once. I will send him away, my lady, if you wish."

"No, I will come," she said calmly. "Georgiana, I will be delayed. Will you pour tea for me?"

Georgiana came over to settle herself happily at the tea table. Only Lady Helena was there, and the two women got along quite nicely.

Lady Mary followed the footman to the small front parlor, the stiff one she remembered from her arrival to the castle. There she found Jeremiah Shaw, standing uneasily in the middle of the room.

"Mr. Shaw. Is Anne unwell? I will come at once—"

"No, no, my lady. It don't be on her account." His sullen face relaxed a trifle. "She and babe are doing well. Ye will come over soon and see him?"

"I shall be happy to come. My husband is away at the time. When he returns, we shall come to visit."

"Yes, yes. That don't be why I asked to see you, my lady." Heavy gloom descended on him once more. He wrung his big hands together, as though unconscious of his gesture. "There be sommit wrong, though, with the Bostwicks, my lady. I said I would come to you, and ye would make it right, and ye could."

"I will try. What is it, Mr. Shaw?" She tried to gesture him to be seated, but he shook his head. He was plainly nervous.

"It be the young lord, Mr. Christopher," he said. "He was drunken and raging this afternoon, and he would never have done it, I feel sure, my lady. But he did, and the damage is done."

"What did he do?" she asked sharply, her mouth setting.

"He come to the Bostwick cottage to survey it, and the land. And Bostwick did tell him about the land being poorly, and the roof leaking, my lady. And Mr. Christopher, he roped the roof, and he pulled it off, and said that would mend matters, and he was going to ride off. But Bostwick, he called after him, some matter about being drunken, and the young lord, he took his shotgun, and he shot all the cows."

"My good Lord above," said Mary, completely exasperated. "The young fool! He is—" She stopped abruptly, her lips tightening over the furious words. She could picture it—Christopher, enraged over her rebuff and sodden with drink, laughing at the misery of a farmer and his family. "The Bostwicks, they are the ones to the south of your farm, with four children?"

"Yes, my lady, they be the ones." Jeremiah Shaw was eyeing her curiously, waiting for her response, his back stiff, his head proud. He was not at all sure she would help, she knew that. He was waiting, holding judgment in suspension.

"The matter shall be made right, Mr. Shaw. Meantime, will you take in the family for a few days, so the weather will not hurt them? Their food will be paid for at once. I will see to it that the roof is mended and the cows replaced. Tell Mr. Bostwick he shall have a visit from me tomorrow morning."

Jeremiah Shaw stared down at her from his great height. Finally he nodded, slowly. "Yes, my lady. It will be done. Thank you, my lady."

She showed him to the door, with the footman hovering anxiously. She had a feeling that the servants knew all about the matter. They were mostly local folk from the village, and she knew the gossip spread like fire among them.

She returned to the tea and settled herself to wait. But Christopher did not come. Nor did he come to dinner, and when she questioned his valet, the man admitted he was lying in bed, quite drunk. Mary decided to wait until morning, though her temper was not improved by the waiting.

She did not see him until midmorning, when he finally came down to a very late breakfast. She entered the dining room, sat down at her place, took another cup of tea, and waited until he had consumed a healthy portion of the food. Then she began.

"Christopher, it has been reported to me about the Bostwick house, how you pulled off the roof and shot the cows."

He glared at her, a small boy with a large headache, and grunted crossly. "What matter? Stephen will settle things later."

"No, we will not wait for Stephen to return," she said, with ominous gentleness. "You will do the mending of this matter. Stephen has enough problems without this. You have done the damage, you will do the mending."

He growled. "You are mad. You don't expect me to mend a roof, do you? I can see me, on top of their little cottage, setting up the flax, or whatever they use."

"No, you would do a bad job of it," she said sharply. "But you will hire the roofers without delay. You will oversee the job, and see it done well, and immediately! You will go to the market and get Mr. Ashwood the innkeeper to help you choose cows to replace the ones you shot. And you will pay all out of your own pocket, Mr. Christopher! And I shall see to it that you do all this at once, and before Stephen returns."

They quarreled angrily. The footman started to come in, backed out hastily, and left them to it. Christopher turned red, argued with her, said it would be humiliating. Mary retorted with great satisfaction that she hoped it would be.

"And furthermore," said Mary, "You will apologize to Mr. and Mrs. Bostwick for the great inconvenience to them, and for your rudeness, and for your ill manners. I shall be there to see that you apologize with grace and completeness!"

"I do not apologize to any damn farmer," said Christopher furiously. "Wait until Stephen comes back! He will have a lot to say about your insolence! He will not endure to have me treated so!"

"While Stephen is gone, I am mistress here, and solely in command," said Mary, with more calm than she felt. "You will do as I say!"

He did, but not amiably. She drove in her carriage, with a groom and footman accompanying her. Christopher raced ahead on his horse, and waited sullenly for her at Shaw's farmhouse. Mary saw them all come out on her approach. She insisted that Christopher make a completely abject apology, to his fury and the farmers' amazement. Then she took Mr. Bostwick into her carriage, and they proceeded to the village. The roofers were hired and told to set to work at once the following morning.

Then they consulted Mr. Ashwood, who kept his face straight, though there was a lively twinkle in his eyes as he promised to help Christopher and Mr. Bostwick choose good cows at the fair on Friday.

At dinner that evening, Christopher gave his mother and his wife a vividly colored account of the day's activities, and enlisted their sympathies. Lady Helena was outraged at Mary, and openly threatened to tell Stephen everyone's opinion of the matter on his return.

"Do that, Lady Helena," said Mary, bitingly. "I am sure he will need to have his eyes opened to your son's behavior. He has indulged the boy shockingly. Christopher needs discipline, and he has not received much to date."

Georgiana burst into tears and left the room. Christopher berated Mary angrily. Lady Helena was cold and rude to her, and both stormed out before the conclusion of the meal. Mary was left to the sweets and wine in solitary comfort. She reflected that it was at least more peaceful this way.

Evan Basset came to join her in the jade sitting room after dinner, as she drank coffee alone. He seemed quite grave, accepting coffee and seating himself beside her on the satin sofa.

"Lady Mary, I will not rebuke you as the others have done. But have you considered the dangers of this course? Christopher is a strong-willed boy, and Stephen has always adored him. You would turn your husband against you, just as you are winning him."

She tightened her lips. "The boy has done wrong. It must be made right," she said quietly.

They spoke for some time of the matter, and of the farms. She was very impressed with his good sense and his sensibility about the people hereabouts. They talked for over an hour before he excused himself to return to his suite of rooms in his private wing of the castle.

The next day was one of the most difficult Mary had ever endured. She forced the sullen, furious Christopher to accompany her again to oversee the roofers—though they knew much more of the matters than either of the castle visitors. While Christopher paced about angrily, Mary went out to the vegetable gardens with plump Mrs. Bostwick and earnestly discussed planting and children and cows, as though nothing else in the world mattered.

Jeremiah Shaw came over several times and watched, returning to his own farm as though the world weighed heavily on him.

At the end of the afternoon, when they had returned to the castle for tea, Christopher turned on Mary savagely. "I hope you are satisfied with my humiliation. I'm going up to London at once! You shall not see me again for a time—"

"Oh, no, Christopher," she said, quite calmly, passing a cup of tea to the trembling Georgiana. "You have work to do here. You have cows to buy on Friday, the roof to oversee, and Stephen asked you to visit two more farms and report on them by the time he returns."

She might as well be hung for a sheep as a lamb, she thought, with some amusement. Christopher argued with her for a short time, then stomped out of the room in a towering rage. She thought he would not soon again ask her for an affair. He must dislike her intensely by now!

But she needed more comfort than that. Lady Helena took her sharply and rudely to task for her behavior toward her beloved son. Georgiana added her words, and the rest of teatime was decidedly unpleasant.

Mary thought of Evan Basset. On impulse, she made her way to the far end of the wing and knocked on the huge door there. It was opened by a valet, a man she saw rarely, since he waited on his master in that suite alone.

"I would like to see Mr. Basset."

He hesitated. Evan came up behind him as she stepped inside. "No one comes here, Lady Mary," he said quite sharply. His face was flushed. "I do not allow—"

But behind him she had caught a glimpse of the huge,

luxurious room. "My land—what—what is this?" she gasped. Her eyes widened. The huge ancient room was full of satin furniture, of paintings of the most glorious colorings, of small wood tables with treasures of jade and teakwood and ivory. Her gaze went from one rare object to another. "Why—Mr. Basset—you live more grandly than—" She stopped abruptly, her eyes returning to study his face.

His face was quite red, his eyes angry. "You had no right to come in here," he snapped. "My late lord gave me these apartments—"

"And all the family treasures?" she asked sharply, pointing to a portrait on the wall. It was a beautiful painting of a woman, Stephen's mother, she knew by the face. Beside it was one of a lord, an older man but the image of Stephen. "Why are his father and mother hanging on the walls of your apartments? And those jewels—" She spotted the small glass-enclosed case on the wall. She went over to them and stared incredulously at the opened boxes from which spilled pearls, diamond necklaces, garnets, rubies, sapphires, emeralds larger and more grand than even the ones Stephen had given to her.

She turned about to look at the silk and velvet furniture, sofas and chairs of dark, polished red wood. Tables inlaid with marble in the most precious designs, their tops covered with statuettes of ivory and gold, boxes of rare carving, porcelain toys and china.

"There are more treasures here than in the whole rest of this castle, Mr. Basset," she said very quietly. "How do you explain this? Is this your pay for years of service to the late lord and the present one?" And she faced him fearlessly.

The red slowly died from his face, leaving him calm and placid once more. A slight smile played on his lips.

"You are shrewd, Lady Mary. I thought you would discover my secret before long, though I had not counted on having so little time to discover your character first. I think, though, that I have it right, and that I may trust you."

"Trust me? Not to tell Stephen you have most of the family treasures in here?" she inquired sharply. "How did you read my character, Mr. Basset? I am not to be bribed to keep still!"

"No, I do not expect that. Let me explain as I show you the lovely gems of my collection." And he actually smiled, as he took her arm and led her over to the jewels in the glass case. "These are the Huntingdon treasures, yes, of course. Would you like to know where I found them? I will tell you—they were on their way in a coach to be sold in London! The late lord cared so little for them, and Lady Helena had expressed a wish for some vulgar trifle, so he was sending them to be sold! I rescued them, sent money instead, and began to save things for the family. I had discovered they cared nothing for the rarest paintings. Let me show you the Reynolds portrait of one of Lord Stephen's ancestors!" And he took her over to it.

She gasped in amazement as he showed her one item after another. Some had been on their way to London or to a dealer to be sold. Some had been rusting in attic rooms. Silver and china had been neglected.

"I have worked for the Huntingdon family since my boyhood, when I was orphaned," he said, finally seating her on a wine velvet couch, and putting a case of beautiful emeralds in her hands to study. "I loved them as my own family. They treated me with careless generosity which was curiously their own. I was one of them, yet not one. I resolved to keep the family treasures in trust for them. And you, Lady Mary, will help me."

She fingered the fine emeralds, the last doubts of him fading. "But—how can I? What can I do, Mr. Basset?"

"Keep the secret," he said simply. "Help me preserve the treasures for the ones who will appreciate them. Stephen does not; Christopher does not. He would sell the St. John crest for a fine horse—don't look at me in such amazement! Didn't you know he sent away the family crest of diamonds and jade to be sold when he wished to purchase a mare? Yes, I have the crest here," and he brought it to her. She sighed and shook her head over it, convinced now against her will.

"And Stephen let him do it?"

"Lord Stephen cares as little for possessions as the late lord did, and Christopher is even worse. Family heirlooms mean nothing. They are impulsive. They would put money into land or horses, or into a gambling trip to Paris. Yes, my late lord and Lady Helena frequently went to Paris to gamble away a fortune, returning as gaily as though they had won!"

"How terribly, willfully extravagant!" she murmured, shocked to the depths of her thrifty Scottish soul at all this revealed to her. "How could they? And yet—they were generous to me. All these dresses, the jewels, the cloaks and fur bonnets—"

"Yes, they are generous, I will say that for them. Too generous. They almost gave away the portrait of Her Majesty Queen Elizabeth to a casual visitor to the castle," he added, wrily, with a little exasperated laugh. "I rescued it by hiding it and pretending it could not be located! So it resides in my bedroom until the time I can restore it. My Lady Mary, forgive me if I am impertinent, but I hope you will teach your sons to be more thoughtful and careful of their heritage! You can do it; I can see that you love and respect these possessions, though they are temporal. I feel they are the visible signs of a great family which has lasted for hundreds of years. Will you help me preserve these treasures?"

She promised, and left the lavishly decorated suite in a very thoughtful frame of mind. Mr. Basset was right, they were wildly extravagant, thinking little of possessions, giving generously to whoever asked. They were willful, daring, adventurous, gambling, moody, secretive, and unexpected, with hidden currents in their natures.

Stephen returned by the time the cows had been purchased and the roof repaired. He was met by Christopher, who had ready his long tale of woe and abuse, and by Lady Helena, who embroidered on the theme. Even Georgiana chimed in to heap wrath on the head of Lady Mary. She took it with outward calm.

After hearing their story, Stephen turned on Mary coldly, his eyes flashing. "I will not have my brother so treated! You did wrong to humiliate him in front of everyone!"

She stiffened and matched him glare for glare. "I was in charge while you were gone, my lord. And he did great wrong to those people who were in our charge! You have spoiled the boy, but he should not allow the spoiling to hurt a family with four small children!"

Stephen stared down at her as she sat on the jade couch, her teacup untouched beside her. "You could have handled it without humiliating the boy," he said, still coldly.

"The boy—is twenty-four, my lord. It is time he assumed some burden of responsibility, not added to the burdens," she said crisply. Inwardly, she was shivering. She did not want Stephen to be angry with her.

Mary said little more to defend herself. She was not sorry she had acted as she had. She was only sorry if it opened a deep gulf between herself and Stephen.

At dinner, Christopher went on about his rage at a great rate, and Lady Helena was crude and cruel, until Stephen finally said, "Enough! No more of this matter. I will see to it tomorrow. Lord God, can't a tired man have any peace?"

And they stopped and let him have his peace, very solicitously, with sideways glances at Mary, silent at her end of the table. They seemed to feel he would take their side completely.

But the next day, Stephen rode out early. When he returned, he was very thoughtful. He called Christopher into his study and talked to him for a long time. The young man emerged white and shaking. Stephen went to Mary's suite of rooms upstairs, where she was working on the estate accounts and the castle books.

She laid aside her pen, not knowing what had transpired at the meeting. Stephen said, looking down at her, "You were right, Mary. I have spoiled the boy. He thought nothing of leaving a family without a roof over their heads. And no cows, when there are two small ones. If you had not acted as you did, they would have been sorely ill. I have spoken to Christopher, and I think he will not be so reckless again."

She was surprised at his decisive words, more surprised that he had decided to take her part in the matter. He smiled his rare, sweet smile at the look on her face.

"Well, my Mary, didn't you think I would see the justice of your actions?" He bent and kissed her cheek warmly. He had not come to her the night before, and she had not known whether he was angry with her or merely weary from his long journey. "Now, tell me what other matters you have been handling in my absence!"

CHAPTER NINE

THERE WAS, nevertheless, a stiffness and coolness in the castle household for a few days. Stephen did not come to Mary at night, and as she lay awake, she wondered if he was indeed angry with her. He was very busy, it was true —but was he too weary to come to her—or too angry with her—or was he becoming bored with her?

She did not know why her heart ached so much at the thought. She only knew she could not sleep well; she tossed and turned and pushed aside the covers, only to draw them up again for warmth and comfort.

She resented the way she had come to depend on him already. She had never meant to let her life become so entangled with that of another, even a husband. And the circumstances of their marriage, a marriage of anger and convenience, had precluded any thoughts of tenderness or love. Yet—there it was.

Stephen asked Mary one night to come with him to a distant farm and gain the confidence of the farmer's wife. He felt sure there was some difficulty there which he could not reach. Mary was flattered at his confidence and eagerly agreed to go. She, Stephen, and Evan Basset discussed the matter that night, and Evan was able to give them some insight into the nature of the farmer and his wife. He thought he man was brooding over the recent death of his eldest son.

"The lad had gone out with the fishermen, though he was only fifteen and he drowned one of the first nights. The man blames himself for letting the lad go and the wife is brooding badly. They scarcely speak to each other or to anyone. The fishing life is hard. He was too young for it, and a frail lad besides."

"I don't know what I can do about it then," sighed Mary, her heart going out to them.

"If anyone can help, you can, Lady Mary," said Evan quietly. Stephen flashed her his sweet smile, and her heart lifted. The two of them had confidence in her, seemed to need her help. Well, she would try.

They took one of the best carriages and Stephen's favorite grays. They made a good trip, visited the farmstead, and came away exceedingly puzzled.

"She would not talk at all to me," said Mary thoughtfully. "Stephen—she seemed actually afraid. Why would she be afraid of me?"

"I don't know, Mary. I don't know." His attention seemed to be on the horses before him, but she knew he was deep in thought.

It was a two-hour ride back to the castle. She settled back to enjoy the good pace and the presence of her husband. They were both silent, preoccupied with their own thoughts. Finally she noticed the darkeneing clouds. "Is night coming so soon, Stephen?"

He lifted his head, glanced about. "Oh, Lord, one of our famous storms," he said, studying the sky. "Mary, we are in for a soaking, I fear. I'll stop and get out one of the rugs." He did so, and they proceeded, but the storm was soon upon them.

It was late evening, turning dusk. The sky was completely dark, and the thunder roared, and the lightning flashed in the western heavens. The horses reared and neighed in fright. Stephen held them firmly, spoke to them commandingly, but his voice was sometimes drowned in the fury of the electrical storm. And then the rains began, descending in sheets of water which soon had them drenched through. Mary held the rugs over their heads while Stephen drove along the now-familiar paths. They were still more than half an hour from the castle.

A particularly brilliant flash of lightning made one of the horses rear up, and the other began to plunge in the traces. Stephen drew them to a slow pace, but it was evident that his wrists were strained in holding them. He was scowling and glancing up now and then at the fury of the storm about them.

"There's no help for it, we have to go by way of the forest paths. Dangerous," he muttered, half to himself.

Mary said nothing, her mouth set. He was with her, they would share the danger. She was amazed at her own coolness. Ordinarily she was terrified of lightning storms.

In the forest, it was so pitch dark that the lightning helped, for Stephen could then see the path. But the horses were full of fright, plunging again and again, thoroughbreds as temperamental as high-strung people. Mary tried to peer ahead into the road, but could make out only a few feet at a time. She frowned, leaned forward. There seemed to be something white ahead—no, it was her imagination—no, she did see something.

"Stephen," she began to say. "There is something—someone—on the—"

The horses reared straight up in fright as a ghostly white figure suddenly appeared in the path ahead of them. They neighed, whinnied, pranced about, pulled forward. The traces broke, and the horses ran wild.

Through the forest, along the path, under the trees, they raced pell-mell. Mary wanted to scream. She clung to Stephen's arm. He was holding the reins, but he had no power over the horses now. He flung them down and clasped Mary's arm, speaking into her ear.

"We'll have to jump for it, Mary. Wait. When I tell you, make sure your skirts are held high and jump out. I'll come back for you. There's a turn in the road—ready—jump, Mary! Mary, jump out!"

He pushed her, and she jumped out to land sprawling and breathless in the path. She felt the pine needles under her outspread hands, felt the jolt in her left wrist as something gave way. The carriage careened around the turn. She lost sight of it. She felt alone, frightened, half-crying with the tension.

Then Stephen came running back to her, knelt beside her. She could not make out his face in the darkness. The rain poured down steadily about them in spite of the thick trees. "Mary—are you hurt? Mary—" She felt his arms urgently about her.

"My wrist—is all—left wrist," she gasped breathlessly.

"My poor love! We'll go to the hunting lodge—it's nearby—come, I'll help you." He drew her up, and they ran through the downpour for a few hundred yards. She thought a shelter had never seemed so welcome as the rustic wood cottage loomed before them.

Stephen pushed at the door and opened it. "Never kept locked," he said briefly, and pulled her in with them.

She sniffed as soon as she was inside. "I smell smoke."

"Smoke. I'll light the fire at once, Mary. You are soaked through! Come, stand near and warm yourself. It will soon be alight." And he knelt at the laid fire in the fireplace, and soon had it ablaze. She noticed that some of the logs were half-burned through, that the fire caught readily, showing there was no dampness. It puzzled her. She sniffed again. Smoke? Yes, tobacco smoke. That was it. She turned to speak to Stephen, but he had gone into the next room.

She followed him. He was in the one bedroom, pulling

back the blankets. "The bed is made, thank heavens for that. Mary, pull off your clothes. Here are towels—dry yourself. And your hair, it is soaked. You'll catch a chill—" And he came to her and helped her unfasten her cloak.

"You're wet too, Stephen. You had better undress—"

"You first. We'll get you dry and in bed. I'll get some tea when we're dry. There should be supplies in the kitchen. We keep the lodge well stocked."

He was helping her unbutton the dress. Her fingers were clumsy, and her left wrist was swollen already. He looked at it, exclaiming over it, his brow clouded.

"You have indeed injured it, Mary. My fault. I should have jumped first and caught you. But you might not have been able to jump out—"

"Don't reproach yourself, Stephen. It was the only way to do it. If I hadn't landed so clumsily, all would have been well," she said practically.

He lifted the dress off her, helped her remove her shifts and undergarments. She saw and felt the burning of his look as he became aware of her. She blushed for herself, yet it was only practical to remove the wet garments. He brought towels and rubbed her briskly until she was warmer.

"Sorry there are no night rails for you," he said, when she was more dry. "Hop into bed, and let me do your hair."

She got into bed, thankful to cover herself with the blankets. He was bending over her, rubbing her hair with a towel.

"Let me do that, Stephen. Remove your wet clothes before you catch a chill yourself."

"I'll do that," he said quietly. He stood up and began to undress. She rubbed at her hair, trying not to watch him. The light from the fire in the next room filtered into the bedroom, and she could see his lean, tanned body, his firm arms and legs, his hairy chest quite clearly. She wanted to turn away, but she could not.

Finally she lay back, spreading her hair on the pillow over the towel. She was weary, her wrist aching. Stephen came over to the bed, a towel about his thighs. "Do you want tea, Mary? Shall I fix—" Then he bent over and slowly drew back the blankets. He looked down, gazing hungrily at her.

"Mary," he said, huskily. "Mary—my own Mary—"

The towel was discarded, and so were thoughts of tea. He slid into bed beside her and took her in his arms. She felt the chill of his flesh turn warm as he pressed himself to her body.

She squirmed. It was so unexpected, his movements were so suddenly passionate. Her arms were pressed against his chest, holding him off a little. She gazed up shyly into the intense sherry-brown of his eyes, made darker by passion.

"After all, we are married," he said, with a little teasing smile. "It is not as though we were having an illicit rendezvous!"

"Are we not?" she asked, dreamily.

"No—we are married—and you belong to me—"

"I thought you had forgotten, my lord!"

"What?" he asked, his mouth against her throat, his tone muffled, deep. She felt his big hands seeking her.

"Milord—I thought you—had forgotten—we were married! You have not visited—my bed—for—oh, Stephen—" And she wriggled about under his hands.

"My Lady Mischief," he said huskily. "My Lady—Mischief! You are always—teasing—and tormenting—me—but you—shall pay—for your—teasing—"

And he bent to her, and made love to her so wildly, so passionately, that she quite forgot the storm that raged outside.

He had never made love to her quite like that before,

she thought, while she could still think.

It was like dancing, when the music and the emotion made one lose all thought of anything in the outside world. When their inner music dictated a driving need to move and dance and turn, and their emotions welled up in unison, and there was no need to say or direct or respond, they were moving as one body.

Instant response to instant need, and heat replying to heat, and time sliding away as though it melted beneath them. The storm raged, Mary could hear it howling about the chimney of the lodge. But it meant nothing. It was nothing. The wind and rain and the lightning and thunder were nothing like the storm inside.

They did not sleep for a long, long time, but it seemed like moments, like seconds. When he finally lay down to rest beside her and drew her into his arms with firm possession, she was content to lie and listen to the wild beating of his heart as it slowed to a peaceful calm. And she went to sleep with that beating in her ear. Like the sea, like the eternal strong sea, against the beach.

CHAPTER TEN

IN THE MORNING, the sun shone as brightly and cheerfully as though it had never dreamed of a storm such as raged the night before. As Mary peered from the window, she saw the loveliness of the rain-freshened forest, the carpets of May flowers in primrose and pink and white, the greening of the forest floor, and the soaked dark brown pine needles. It looked like a beautiful world.

Stephen brought her clothes to her and helped her dress. She was clumsy, her left wrist very swollen and useless. He kept looking at her as he helped her put on the dried undergarments, then slid the dress over her head and buttoned it carefully for her. She had bathed in hot water he had brought, and he had insisted, in a most loverlike way, in helping her with that also, though she blushed and protested.

Her red curly hair was a tangle. She found a comb in her reticule and tried to bring some order to it. But the swollen left wrist and her stiff left shoulder would not permit it. Stephen, already dressed, watched her for a few moments.

"Here, let me try," he said finally, and took the comb

from her. He drew it slowly through the tangle, pulled strands apart carefully, worked with it so gently she felt no tugging at all. When it was in shining order again, he said, "Will you try to bind it up?"

She winced as she tried to lift her left arm and shook her head. "I'll leave it down, I believe, Stephen. There's no one to see me here."

"Except me—and I love your hair all shining down about you," he said, and cupped her face in his hands under the hair. He looked down into her face, seemed to study it intently, then bent and kissed her mouth very slowly and deeply.

It was then that she knew. She knew she loved him. Wildly, completely, unquestioningly. She loved him, though she did not know him, did not understand him, resented his domination, fought him when she could. She loved him with all the force and fervor and crazy devotion in her whole small body.

How had it happened, she wondered, lost in dream, as he kissed her hungrily. Had she loved him when she first saw his cold, hard, haughty look? Had she wanted to melt him then?

Or had it been later, when she had experienced his kindness and generosity? When she was ill, when he came devotedly to see her, and looked down at her, and brushed her red hair back from her forehead, and asked how she felt? Had it been when he protected her from Christopher's teasing and the slights of the other two women, so unobtrusively that she had scarcely realized he was doing so?

Or had it been only when she had experienced his lovemaking, found him so tender and gentle in bed, yet so possessive? When had she first yielded completely to him? She did not know.

The love had been planted in her and had grown in darkness, and she had not known it was there until now, when it flowered and bloomed. A Scottish rose, blossoming, he had said, and now she felt it.

"I hate to leave here," Stephen was whispering to her between kisses on her cheeks and throat. "We are—completely alone—here—I like this. I like being alone with you, Mary, my Mary. No one to interrupt—no other being in the world but us—"

She wanted to reply, but she could not. Her love was unspoken; she felt shy and afraid to say anything which might break the spell. When he released her, gently, she turned slowly from him and brushed back her hair in an uncertain gesture.

"I'll fix some tea," said Stephen, more practically. "Then we'll start to walk back. We might get a ride with some farmer."

"Yes—we might—get a ride," she managed to say as she walked before him into the next room, conscious of him behind her, knowing he was looking at her as she walked.

They drank tea and ate a couple of the dried biscuits which were about all the cupboards contained. Then she put on her cloak, lifted the hood about her head, and they started out. Stephen put his arm about her to help her over the roughness of the path.

They walked along slowly. The sun had risen higher in the sky, and the warmth was making the chillness of early morning recede. She noticed the yellow primroses on the fence on the border of a farm; they seemed brighter than usual. The patches of wild violets, peeping in purple shyness from their green leaves, seemed more beautiful than any other spring she had known. And the tiny wild pink and white windflowers were more dainty and more delicate than she had ever remembered.

So this was love—the magic which made the world seem so much more beautiful! Love painted the spring more brightly, and glowed the heavens more brilliantly, and gave extra sparkle to the dewdrops on the vivid green grass. Love made an arm feel precious, and a voice more tender and clear, and every memory something to catch the breath.

"How far is it?" she asked, not really caring, wishing the walk would never end.

"About two or two and a half hours of walking, Mary. However, I hope there will be wagons on the road before long." And he looked ahead, a slight frown on his dark face. "Are you very weary, my love?"

"No, not weary at all, I slept well," she said, and stupidly blushed. He looked down in time to see the reddening of her cheeks, and he touched her face with his free hand.

"I should apologize for last night," he murmured, mischief in his sherry eyes. "I should have let you rest. But you must blame yourself too—for being too sweet to leave!"

"Stephen!" she murmured. Her face turned from his for a moment, his eyes were so brightly knowing, so intimate. He laughed softly.

Her breath came more quickly and she felt a tightness in her chest, a pounding of her heart.

Both heard the horses at the same moment and looked ahead toward the bend in the road. A carriage swept around the curve toward them, the two horses galloping magnificently.

"Evan Basset," said Stephen, his tone colorlessly quiet. "Good. We shall not have to walk."

Mary was conscious of both relief and keen disappointment. She did not mind walking, and she had looked forward to this long walk with Stephen. Now a third person would be there, and the sweetly mischievous teasing would stop. The formality would return, and the night would be forgotten—by Stephen. She knew that she herself would never forget it.

Evan Basset pulled up beside them, tied the reins to the post, and climbed down. There was great relief in his face, and he began questioning them at once.

"Where have you been? What happened? When I was told the horses had returned this morning, I was terrified. That storm last night—were you out in it?"

"Easy, easy, Evan," said Stephen calmly, holding up one large palm. "Let's get Mary home. She has had quite an ordeal, and her wrist is very swollen." He lifted Mary up into the carriage, then swung in beside her. Evan waited until they were settled, then took his place beside Stephen and picked up the reins.

"What did happen?" he asked more quietly. "When I heard that Thunder and Star had come home, the carriage almost torn from the traces, I was worried sick. Was it an accident?"

Stephen hesitated so slightly that Mary thought she was mistaken in his pause. "Yes, of course. The lightning frightened the horses. When a particularly bad bolt came, they broke free and went careening along. I had Mary jump out, then I jumped and went back to her. I found she had a hurt wrist and was jolted about. I remembered the hunting lodge, and we made a run for it in the rain."

"You must have been soaked through!" Evan exclaimed. "I wonder that you don't have a chill!"

"We soon got warm and dry," said Stephen without expression. "We lit the fire in the lodge, and there were blankets."

"Good thing. How about food? Or tea?"

"Tea, but little food. The cabin should be supplied, Basset."

"Right. I'll see to it."

While the men talked, Mary was thinking. She had definitely smelled tobacco smoke last night. And there had been a fire in that lodge fireplace not long before.

And another detail bothered her. "I am surprised that the horses only returned this morning. The way they were traveling," she said innocently, "I would have thought they would be back in their own stables in double-quick time, within half an hour, last night."

There was a slight pause. Mary could not see Basset's face. She glanced up toward Stephen's dark profile; he was gazing straight ahead, as though only the distant vista interested him.

"Oh—the horses," said Evan. "Yes, the grooms finally told me they had returned last night. You may be sure I rebuked them for not calling me at once. Of course, I was out until after midnight myself, on horseback—the Frazer family, my lord, you will recall."

"Yes, oh, right. How are they?"

"Badly, I'll make a full report to you later today. But I was not told about the horses until this morning, when I went out to the stables. When I saw the condition of the carriage, and then learned neither of you had returned, I was quite shocked. The butler was remiss. He should have sent grooms out."

"I will speak to Wenrick," said Stephen without expression.

"He has grown careless of late," said Basset in a hesitant tone. "I have found him slow to respond to orders and remiss in some matters. I will speak to him myself if you wish, my lord."

"I will attend to it," said Stephen. "You have enough to do, Basset. You must not be responsible for every detail. You will make my gratitude an immense weight on me," he said, and smiled slightly.

Mary grew silent; she leaned back in the circle of Stephen's protective arm, and let the men speak of other matters. She was intent in thought.

The horses had returned to the stables last night—but no one had sent out for the missing passengers of the wrecked carriage. And Wenrick was more careful and concerned; he was not careless.

Evan Basset had said at first that the horses had not returned last night. Then he said that he had not been notified that they had returned last night. Which statement was true? Was he protecting someone?

Stephen had told Basset that the lightning had frightened the horses. It had, but it was the ghostly white figure that had sent them thundering home, breaking the traces. Why had he not mentioned that white figure? Had he not seen it? Or did he choose not to tell Basset about it?

And that tobacco smoke in the lodge. The fire which had been lit and extinguished. The lack of food in the lodge. Someone had been there before them, been there for a long time, perhaps hours.

Waiting? Waiting for them?

A little chill of fear and suspicion went up her straight Scottish spine.

Someone had set out to kill them and had almost succeeded.

If she had been alone, or if Stephen had not thought quickly enough, the horses would have wrecked the carriage, and them in it. They might have been thrown out, their necks broken.

Killed.

CHAPTER ELEVEN

MARY GLANCED AGAIN at Stephen's face. It was not her imagination, she thought from her end of the long shining table. Stephen was upset about something. She knew that grave preoccupied look, that darkening of the sherry eyes.

The guests noticed nothing. Evan Basset was being charming to Georgiana, and the girl, who had gained more self-confidence in her marriage, was responding with an unaccustomed sparkle and wit. Christopher was lazily watching them, a little smile on his lips as they exchanged banter. Lady Helena was holding forth to her favorite friend, Mrs. Demerest. Squire Demerest was alternately watching his only daughter Georgiana and gazing down at the lovely, sparkling face of another guest, a friend of Georgiana from London.

Things had been surprisingly peaceful the past few days. Mary's wrist was healing slowly, and though her shoulder had given her more pain than she had expected, that also was mending. Otherwise, the only aftereffects of their mishap were Mary's worries about her and Stephen's safety.

Did Stephen know or guess that someone had tried to

kill them? She had not discussed it with him. She had started to several times, but some ring of warning had stopped her. Stephen was two persons, the ardent lover and a strange, brooding man with a frown who gave curt commands. She never knew which one he would be.

I don't know him, I don't know him at all, she thought, and then caught his glance down the long table shining with china, fragile glass, the silver epergne brilliant with red and yellow and white roses.

He gave her a slow smile, an intimate look that could make her blush even at a large dinner party. She glanced away again and caught the friendly twinkle in Evan Basset's eyes. He knew how she felt, she thought, and she was a little comforted. Evan Basset had accepted her from the first.

The others had not, did not even now. She saw Lady Helena glance at her, then away, her nose up. She was a strange woman, thought Mary, not for the first time. She could be friendly, nice, giving advice freely whether wished or not. Other times, she was cold, aloof, making cutting remarks about Mary's unsuitable background, her inability to manage a castle and its household, her poor appearance as a hostess. She managed to convey the impression that under her grooming, Georgiana would have made a much better lady than Mary.

Mary thought sometimes she would give it all up for a quiet cottage with Stephen. She looked down at the shining white porcelain plate with a decorated border of bright red roses and green leaves. But Stephen was Stephen Huntingdon, Lord St. John, master of the Castle of St. John, and she was technically its mistress. And so there was no other course.

She must manage somehow. She must learn and struggle, and hold up her head, and secretly ask advice from Mrs. Ramsey.

There was something else that cut. Lady Helena had

said several times recently that Stephen was accustomed to invite guests from London and the country around. He had not invited anyone since his marriage. Was it because Stephen was ashamed of the management of the castle, ashamed of his governess-bride?

He had married her to save his pride. Was he regretting the bargain? Did he enjoy her body—but feel ashamed of her manners and herself?

She kept her head lowered as a wave of shame and regret swept over her. She had shown him pretty plainly that she enjoyed him, that she liked his lovemaking. But he had never said that he loved her, so she had never said it either. And now—now that she was doubting him, doubting whether he really wanted to be married to her, it was all the worse.

She had her pride also, she thought, her fierce Scottish pride in her birth. But it was true—she had been maid and nursery governess and girl-of-all-work for the Evertons. She had come here with ten guineas given to her to marry a man who had not waited for her. No wonder Stephen was ashamed for his fine friends to meet her.

The only guests they had in their home were from the village, or friends of the squire and the vicar. Mary raised her head as the butler paused beside her. She nodded, as he whispered something about serving the next course. Again, her dreaming had caused neglect of her guests, she thought, as Lady Helena sent her a severe look. The woman was frivolous and flighty, but she thought highly of the social amenities, and a five-minute delay in serving a course was a serious matter to her.

Mary was glad to leave the table as they retired to the jade drawing room. She served coffee to the ladies, and when the gentlemen joined them, she poured the sherry and brandy for them. She took refuge in her position behind the coffee tray, directing the footman in a low tone, not conversing with the ladies except in brief words.

She was not one of them. She would never belong, she thought, in sudden desolation.

When Stephen told her that night that he was going away for a few days again, it seemed the bad climax of a bitter evening. She turned her face from him as she sat at the dressing table, brushing her red-gold hair a final time before retiring with him.

"Oh—really?" she said dully. "Where, Stephen?"

She noticed his slight hesitation, took note of it, though why she did not know then. "Oh—to the west, Mary. I have some properties there which have been neglected. In fact, my father had little time or strength to do much with several outlying pieces of land. I must decide whether to settle an overseer or send Evan or Christopher to tend to them. They should not be allowed to go on as they are."

"Of course, Stephen." She noticed he did not say which property or where. She wondered in a sudden flash of jealousy if he had a mistress somewhere and crept off to see her.

He noticed it, she knew, by the way he lifted her up and pressed her to him and moved more slowly with her, giving her time to respond. "Mary, are you weary?" he finally murmured.

"No—no, Stephen." She moved, lifted her arms about his neck, and clung to him, tears clinging to her lashes. She hoped he would not notice she was crying. She would miss him badly.

He left early the next morning, riding his favorite black stallion. She watched him go. He turned to wave, and she waved back, then returned to her duties with determination. She would work hard and make the days pass quickly.

It worked for a couple days. She worked so hard that Mrs. Ramsey was concerned and begged her not to overdo, especially with her wrist still swollen.

It was three days later when Bonny came to her in her bedroom. It was late afternoon, almost time for tea, and

Mary was wondering whether to change to a white muslin or a pink-ribboned green one. The pink, oddly enough, was charming with her red-gold hair; it was a soft pale rose color, like the roses in the garden. Should she wear that one—or wait to wear it when Stephen returned? She wondered again where he was, what he was doing, if he missed her, or if he had feminine consolation.

Bonny murmured to her furtively, sending her a deeply troubled look. "My lady, there is one—one who would —speak with you, please."

"Where, Bonny? In the drawing room?" Mary prepared to get up, thinking it was some trouble on the estate.

"No—no, my lady. Oh, please, don't think the worst of me—I agreed because I—I am worried sick—oh, please see him—"

Mary stared at the maid, noticing her pale face and the hands that worked at each other. "What is it, Bonny?" she asked gently. She wondered if the girl had gotten into trouble. She was hard-working, went out little, seemed so serious. But sometimes— "Are you ill, do you feel sick?"

The girl started and blushed. "Oh, no, my lady, it's not that! It isn't me—no, no. It's a man—would see you. To-night. Please, in the garden near the cliffs. With no one to know."

Mary frowned. Was Christopher still trying to arrange a rendezvous? She would give him a box on the ears that would send all such thoughts flying, she thought crossly.

"What man?" she asked coldly.

"Please, my lady," Bonny whispered. "It be Jeremiah Shaw. He has sommit to tell you, to ask you. But it mun be secret."

When Bonny lapsed into her drawl, Mary knew it was serious. The child was conscientious about talking properly.

"Jeremiah Shaw. I see. All right. What time and where?"

Bonny relaxed; her hands fluttered a moment. "I'll

take you to him, and stand by, my lady. It be after dark, at the cliff, near the old pine. Ye'll go, then?"

"Yes, I'll go."

She gave a deep sigh. "I'll get word to him, then. I promised I'd ask. Oh—and none must know of it! There be trouble, sad trouble, if ought find oot—"

"I'll tell no one," said Mary firmly, and wondered why she promised so easily.

She served tea, talked with the few guests, waited, attended to dinner, served there, waited more and more impatiently for the moment to leave them. She finally excused herself, murmuring something about sleep, and left.

In her room, she changed to her darkest gray dress and put her old black cloak over her, pulling up the hood to hide her red hair. Bonny came to her and furtively led her down a back way, along the dark kitchen alleys, into the stable yards, and out into the gardens.

They crept along the sides of the castle. Inside she could hear Christopher's drawl; beyond the open French windows, she heard Georgiana speaking, laughing a little. Lady Helena's laugh tinkled out. They talked and laughed more freely, thought Mary, when she herself was not there. Bonny led her deeper into the gardens, past the roses and tulips.

And out to the cliffs, where the stark pine loomed against the white chalk cliffs. Where Jeremiah Shaw waited, a dark figure in work clothes, leaning against a stump.

She realized he was sitting down, sprawled there. She hesitated. He whispered, "If ye will but sit down, my lady. I mun talk and you mun listen a spell. If ye will—" And his dark hand indicated the grass beside him.

"I'll wait back here," whispered Bonny, and faded into the darkness behind them.

Mary seated herself on the grass. She was feeling more and more unreal. "What is it? Is it Anne?"

But she knew it was not.

He shook his head. His teeth gleamed a little in the darkness in a brief smile. "No, she and the babe be fine. I had to warn you, for I can't warn my lord. I ain't sure of him, my lady."

A chill went over her. "Tell me."

He shifted a little. "That accident to you and my lord, there in the carriage," he murmured, so his voice would not carry. "It warn't no accident."

There was a pause. She said quietly, "I thought not. I saw a ghostly white figure, which terrified the horses. If we had not jumped out, we might have been killed. How did you know?"

"Talk," he said, briefly. "I hear talk. Danger. My lady, ye be in a mite of danger. It be bad. Ye be in the way of sommun, I be thinking."

"In someone's way? Whose way? Who is trying to kill us?" She clutched his sturdy arm.

He patted her hand soothingly. "I don't know yet, my lady. When I know, I'll be telling you. But they won't talk to me."

"They? Who?"

"Smugglers," he said.

She caught her breath. She thought. "It is—it is something to do with the smuggling, then? The casks and kegs in the castle? The brandy and French wines—"

"And the tea and tobaccy coming in, and the gold going out," he said simply.

She sat there, feeling more and more chilled. The wind was rising off the sea; she could hear the steady pounding.

He whispered, "There be smuggling tonight. I go to watch. I want to see who be in it. Before, I kept away. What I didn't know didn't hurt me, I was thinking. But that is wrong. They keep after me, wanting to take my horses, telling me to leave my stables unlocked. They threaten my missus and my young ones. They be trying to hurt me. Well, I'll get something on them, and they won't be so bold about it!"

"They are—smuggling—tonight?" she whispered aghast.

"Yes, my lady. Down by the other cliffs, about a half mile from here. The way the tides are, it be tonight. I seen the ships coming in this afternoon. I wanted to warn you tonight, because if they catch me tonight, I can't warn you tomorrow."

A frozen wave of horror went through her. He was saying in his understated, quiet way that he might be killed tonight. He meant to fight them, with any weapon he could use to his hand. He meant to get the smugglers in the act, to catch them, to observe them, to threaten them in turn. It was a very dangerous business.

But if she could see them, and tell Stephen—surely he, with his connections could stop the smugglers from attacking Jeremiah and Anne Shaw and their family. And she and Stephen were under attack also. She would see them, would tell Stephen—

"Take me with you," she said, decisively, and we will both observe. We must be very quiet, and stay unobserved ourselves. Then we will know who is doing the smuggling and be able to take measures. We can report them to the law—"

"No—no, my lady—not you—ye cannot go—" His voice rose in its agitation, and she hushed him.

"We will go get evidence and, if we can, I will present the evidence to my husband when he returns. The law should know about this. I don't want you confronting them, Jeremiah. There will be many of them—"

He hung his head and said sullenly, "They be threatening me and mine! They can't do this."

"I know—I know. But a man alone can do little. We must organize to defeat them. Together we can be strong! Surely not all of them are willing to help in the smuggling.

Aren't some of them pressed into the service?"

"Aye, many of them, too many. But they will not tell and go to prison."

"Then we must observe. When were you going to start?"

"When the moon dims. See, it is clouding over now."

They sat quietly, waiting. He seemed to accept the fact that Mary meant to go with him. She, in her turn, felt like she was in a nightmare, a horrible fantasy from which she might not waken. What was she getting into? If only Stephen were home, and she could consult him— But if he *were* home, *would* she consult him?

Jeremiah touched her arm fleetingly. "We go now," she whispered. "I'll send Bonny back to the castle, if ye will trust yourself alone with me."

"I trust you," she said firmly. He nodded and went like a black ghost to where the girl waited. They whispered, and Bonny drifted away. Mary found herself wondering how often the girl had come out and met one of the villagers here, not for romance, but for more serious business, news of the murders, warnings.

She stood up, shaking out her gray skirts and black cloak. She felt stiff from sitting in the damp grass. But she must forget everything now except the need for caution. She followed Jeremiah back into the trees, away from the cliff edge, about half a mile or so.

As they came closer to the chalk cliffs where an inlet curved, and small boats frequently docked, Jeremiah motioned her to crouch. She began to distinguish the murmur of voices, the creak of wagons. She heard the tramp of boots. Jeremiah grabbed her arm and pulled her down abruptly.

She went flat in the grass, lying full length. When her courage returned, she raised her head cautiously. They were near the edge of the cliff, so they could peer down into the inlet and beach below.

As her eyes became accustomed to the scene, she began to distinguish the objects. A large boat with sails lay out beyond the inlet. Nearer were several smaller boats, busily going back and forth between the beach and the ship. Men in dark clothes worked silently rowing and unloading, passing bulky packages across to others on the beach. She saw kegs so huge that a tall man bent under their bulk. Huge brandy flasks, she thought, kegs of wine and ale and French brandy, all smuggled in. Packages of tobacco and tea. And smaller packages being counted out carefully by several men around a minute fire on the beach, their dark, swarthy faces hidden by black scarves and black hats.

Jeremiah was watching intently, trying to identify the men, as she herself was. But they were so bundled up in their greatcoats and work smocks, their scarves and hats, that she recognized no one.

Presently Jeremiah touched her arm, pointed to the side. She nodded. Very carefully they got up on hands and knees and crawled a number of yards to another point, nearer the cliff path. It was dangerous, but both felt the need to see the men struggling up the cliff path with the cargoes to load on the wagons waiting there.

They sank down again in a spot behind several thick bushes. She scratched her face on one low-lying bush, but would not even whisper her distress. The men were walking close to them, some within three yards of their hiding place. Jeremiah had his head up, his dark face alert and sullen, as he watched for familiar faces.

Then she began to see them. Under the shadows of the hats, she saw the familiar faces. A farmer she knew, from one of Stephen's farms. A man from the village. The grocer's assistant. The boy who ran errands in the inn. Two men from the blacksmith's. They were groaning under the weights of the kegs and bulky packages. They carried them to the wagons where other men waited to load them, then drove off with the heavy draft horses.

Now she understood why Jeremiah's orders were to keep his stables unlocked at night. They wanted his horses to work. He had a famous team of sturdy draft horses. They were badly in need of horses tonight! They had huge loads to disperse across the countryside, hide from the customs agents, and deliver to customers in far places.

Then one man stepped close to them, his huge boots tramping. Mary shrank down, her face bent to the ground. She saw the boots coming, heard the man curse roughly as his load shifted.

Jeremiah caught her arm, ready to yank her out of the way. The keg shifted on the burly shoulders; the man cursed angrily. Someone came to him and caught the keg just as it would have fallen.

"Watch that—expensive stuff," said the voice, and the two of them went on.

Mary could scarcely breathe. They had almost been caught. Her chest felt heavy from the pounding of her heart. She opened her lips to let the breath come sighing out instead of gasping. Beside her, she heard Jeremiah breathing heavily, his head down on his arms.

When they were alone again, Jeremiah put his head close to Mary's. "I'm going back—see if it is clear—we best leave. I seen enough. You, too?"

She nodded, whispered, "Yes. We must—go—"

"Wait here, I come back for you." And he was off, slithering over the ground. She pressed herself close to the earth, resting after the fright.

Then she heard another sound, lighter boots, more delicate, more stealthy. She raised her head cautiously—saw a man coming up the cliff path with no bundle. His head was up alertly; he was peering into the darkness steadily. Even under the unfamiliar hat, she recognized him—

Stephen!

She almost cried out his name. She pressed her hand convulsively over her betraying mouth and nearly gagged. She watched, wide-eyed. There was no mistake. It was her husband.

Stephen, walking up the cliff path with no bundle on his shoulders. Stephen, walking lightly, alertly, confidently, as he would in his own garden.

And why not? This was his land, this was his cliff!

She felt a sharp pain in her chest. She wanted to cry, to plead with him, to beg. Instead she lay numbly, frozen with pain and shock. Stephen. One of them. And because of his nature, he was probably one of the leaders. Maybe the leader of them all.

And he walked here, alone and free, watching, observing.

Off on a trip to one of his distant properties— Oh, dear loving kind God, she thought, in agony. Stephen, the leader of the smugglers; the same man she had come to love.

Stephen, in whose arms she had lain, loving him. Adoring him for his gentleness and tenderness, for his sweet lovemaking with her.

And he had ordered murders! She thought of the men who had died. She thought of the threats to Jeremiah Shaw and his wife Anne and their children.

Stephen—could he rescue Anne and help in her birthing one week and order them cruelly to obey or die the next? What was he? Man or devil? Could he murder? Could he order murder done? Was the money from smuggling so much to him? Why? Did he love adventure? Yes, she knew he did. Would he do it for the adventure and excitement of it?

She lay watching her beloved walking past, his boots light and stealthy on thc cliff path, watched him until he had gone up toward the wagons and had disappeared around the bend in the road.

She started violently when something touched her foot. She twisted about. It was Jeremiah, reaching out for her, his face anxious. He beckoned.

She relaxed a little, began crawling backward toward him. He motioned her to crawl on and on, for a long distance, back toward the way they had come, following a twisting course, in and out of the bushes, away further from the cliff edge.

He got her back to the castle. The moon was gone, but from the fresh rising wind and the lightening in the east, she thought it must be close to dawn. They had been out a long time. An eternity, she thought somberly.

Jeremiah escorted her to the back door of the castle. Not even the cooks were stirring yet. Bonny was there, unlocking the door for them, her face drawn and anxious. She obviously had not slept while they were gone.

Jeremiah pressed Mary's hand in a hard, convulsive gesture. "Thank you, my lady," he whispered. "We will talk again—what to do. I saw such men tonight—I never knew they was in it—"

"Many of them unwillingly, Jeremiah," she whispered back. "We must think, we must ponder this carefully, whom—we can—trust—"

He frowned down at her, nodded. He was gone, and Bonny led her weary mistress up the tangle of hallways and back hall and stairs to the wing where her rooms were. In her own suite, Mary stood, arms limp, in the gorgeous drawing room and stared about her. It was unreal, fantastic, what she had seen that night.

"Bonny, I'll take a hot bath and go to bed. When any ask for me, tell them I was ill in the night, and wakeful. I will sleep late today. Tell Mrs. Ramsey and the others nothing. I trust you with my life and Jeremiah's," she added, warningly.

The village girl nodded, her face drawn and hard. "Yes, my lady. Ye are good to us. We are trusting you with our lives also. We must not fail each other," she said, as sturdily as a Scottish free lady would have said it.

They nodded, both of them, the Cornish girl and the Scottish girl. They understood each other. They lived by the same code of honor.

Mary went to bed, but not to sleep for a time. She had much to ponder, including a new, sharp pain in her heart. Her husband was out there, not on his journey to a far estate, but there, with the smugglers.

CHAPTER TWELVE

TWO DAYS LATER, Stephen returned from his "journey," and Mary tried to accept normally his brief account of the state of the distant properties.

He was lying to her, she knew, since she had seen him with her own eyes with the smugglers on the clifftop.

She tried to act naturally, but the constraint showed. He looked at her in a puzzled manner now and then, when she was particularly stiff and formal. She worried about what to do. If she went to the law, she must betray her own husband.

And the law might be paid to look the other way. In which case, both she and Jeremiah Shaw were in deep trouble, for they would disappear, murdered with no one the wiser, no one to care.

She sighed deeply. Stephen turned to her, as she sat on the sofa, her head bent over some accounts.

"Mary, you sound weary of the matters! Why not let them rest for now? Come for a walk with me in the gardens."

She tried to smile, and shook her head. "This must be

finished by noon. Mrs. Ramsey will be going to the village this afternoon—"

"I refuse to be bound by any such rigid schedules!" he said and laughed down at her, coaxing her with him out into the gardens. The sun shone radiantly on the rose bushes, on the freshly turned earth where the gardeners were planting more flowers for the summer.

They strolled and talked. He had his arm about her freely.

He pointed to one bush of radiant yellow roses. "There, that is how you look to me, Mary," he said softly. "All sunshine and beauty."

She blushed and turned her face from him. He put his finger under her chin, turned her face back to his. She looked up into his eyes, finding them darkly passionate and beautiful. Could such eyes lie to her? She studied them intently as he bent closer. Then she closed her own eyes as his light kiss touched her mouth.

She felt again the wondrous thrill going through her. He had only to look at her, touch her, kiss her lightly, and she was helplessly his.

He lifted his head, drew her onward through the gardens. "The ball at the squire's will be amusing, I think. What shall you wear, my Mary? The yellow gown?"

"If you—like, Stephen," she said, hesitating. She had worn it several times.

"What would you rather wear? I like that one."

"Oh—I had thought perhaps—but it is as you wish."

"No, tell me what you want."

"That new emerald green one you had sent from London last week," she blurted out, flushing. "Green is more —becoming to me." And this green gown was of the lightest, fluffiest material, floating about her, of the deep emerald she loved, decorated with sparkling stones and pearls. The skirts were full and floating, the bodice beautifully tight, the waist petite and asking for hands to meet about it.

"I don't see how anything could be more becoming than the yellow, but I am willing to put the matter to the test," he said lightly, smiling down at her. "I had forgotten ordering the green. Was it long in coming?"

"About two weeks, my lord," she said, muffled. Why had he forgotten? More important matters on his mind? Smuggling, murder? Or a mistress? A deep flash of jealousy went through her again. Did he lie to her also about where he went, whom he saw?

" 'My lord!' Why do you call me 'my lord'?" he asked, amused, his arm tightening about her waist. Just then a sharp voice behind them made them both start.

Lady Helena called to them, "This is not seemly!"

They turned about and waited while she came up to them. Her cold stare seemed to pierce Mary.

"What is not?" asked Stephen as though quite bewildered.

Lady Helena nodded at them. "Walking together—with your arm about her—like a footman and his girl walking in a London park!"

Stephen burst into a roar of laughter. His arm tightened when Mary would have pulled away. "Why not? Must only footmen love their girls? Why shouldn't I walk in my own gardens, with my arm about my own wife? Isn't she as pretty as any girl? No, Mary, don't pull away! The hell with seemliness! I waited years for a girl like you to marry me. Now I have her, I'll walk where and when I please with her, ma'am," he added to his stepmother, a devilish twinkle in his eyes, making him seem years younger.

She shook her head severely, the action a contrast to the frivolous bubble of blonde hair on her aging forehead. Conventions were more important to her than anything—except her deep love for her only son, thought Mary. She spent hours teaching Georgiana this and that, the correct way of walking, speaking, greeting. The content of the conversation did not matter, only the manner in which it was spoken.

"We were talking of the squire's ball," said Stephen, more placatingly. "Come, Mother, tell us who is to be there. You will know all the gossip."

She softened a trifle, and consented graciously to take a turn in the gardens with them. Between relating bits of gossip about the coming event, she sent shafts of criticism at Mary for the state of the roses, the neglected bushes near the lake, the trees near the cliff which needed tearing out and replacing.

Mary loved the wild bushes, the trees shaped by the furious winds off the sea, and had no intention of replacing or tearing out any but dead ones.

She listened in silence, nodded her head, and resolved to do as she thought best. But she wished Lady Helena had not come along to spoil her pleasure with Stephen. His arm had finally dropped from her waist, and his hand only loosely held her arm as they walked along. She felt neglected and ignored as the two of them talked easily.

Lady Helena had been mistress of the castle for so many years, it was probably a great effort for her to give up the position, Mary decided, trying to be charitable and understanding. She had probably thought Stephen would never marry, that her own son Christopher would inherit. She had approved of Christopher's marriage to a wealthy and a sweetly manageable girl. That would mean she would continue to be mistress of the castle, to carry herself grandly, to be the sole arbiter of events and social position. But now with Mary there, married to Stephen as Lord of St. John, Lady Helena was severely out of place, and the woman resented it more and more. It was evident in her manner and her speech.

She was still very sharp with Mary, showing her displeasure with her in many ways. She was petty in her criticism. Whenever she could, she told her how she herself would have handled a matter. Mary took the advice as calmly as she could and used what she felt sensibly was correct, freely discarding the remainder. She found she needed her Scottish humor more than ever. She would be swept away on a sea of protocol and grandeur, if she did not call a halt to some of Lady Helena's ideas.

But it was painful, nevertheless, to listen to her strictures on what was proper, what ought to be accomplished, how clumsy the maid was whom Mary was training, how Mrs. Ramsey had neglected her yesterday.

At least the ball was a happy occasion. Mary finally wore the emerald green dress and earned Stephen's immediate approval. He came to her room while she was having her hair brushed and dressed high on the back of her neck and head. "Let me see you, Mary—yes, I do like that! You are beautiful!"

She blushed at his praise and stood up and twirled around with a laugh to hide her embarrassment. "Do you approve of me, my lord?" she asked demurely.

"I am not sure that I do," he said solemnly. Bonny opened her eyes wide in shock. He laughed. "No, I do not! All the young blades will wish to dance with her, and I want to keep her for myself! No, you look entirely too pretty tonight. Isn't there something one could do? Shall I muss your hair?" And he reached out teasingly for the carefully set rolls of curls. Bonny gave a little screech of alarm at the thought that her handiwork was about to be ruined, and Stephen roared with laughter.

"No, no, Stephen, I shall not be ready in time if you muss my hair," said Mary more sedately, and seated herself at the mirror again. The full skirts took some managing, and she settled them carefully. But they would puff up again, billowing in beautiful whirls of deep green silk dotted with the shining green and pearl stones.

Stephen had brought the Huntingdon emeralds with

him, and opened the velvet cases and arrayed her in a glorious necklace of pearls and emeralds. The pendant was a huge emerald as big as a pigeon's egg, shining and sparkling as it lay on Mary's throat. He added a huge ring to her right hand, a bracelet on her left arm, and let her put the long, dangling emerald earrings on her tiny ears.

"You should have your portrait painted this way, Mary," he said, and bent and kissed the place where the gown fell from her white shoulder. Her portrait. She thought of it, and realized suddenly that the portrait of Angela Tarrant was gone from its place.

It had disappeared, and she had not realized until this moment that it no longer hung in the drawing room where she had first seen it. Lovely Angela Tarrant, blonde and blue-eyed, in her beautiful blue satin gown. She was gone. When had the portrait come down? Mary wrinkled her forehead, trying to think why she had not noticed it was gone, and realized that in its place was a landscape of some innocuous English scene.

Stephen placed her green velvet cloak tenderly about her shoulders, and led her away. They were alone in their carriage on the way to the squire's huge residence on the edge of the village. The others had gone ahead in another carriage. With the ladies' huge skirts, there would not be nearly enough room in one, Lady Helena had declared as positively as though she had discovered universal truth.

Stephen commented on it laughingly, and added, to Mary alone, as they rode, "Besides, I would rather be alone with you. Have I told you how beautiful you are?"

She tried to be as light and teasing as he was, though her heart beat hard. "La, sir, I fear not. Ye must think me plain and dowdy, ye have not said I was beautiful!"

"Not more than twice a day since we married," he said, and possessively took her hand in his. He stripped off the thin glove and put the hand to his lips, his warm mouth brushing over and over her fingers and then her palm. "I am much remiss, I apologize, my Mary. I shall tell you four times a day how beautiful you are. Very lovely—very soft and silken—," he added, in a deeper, more passionate tone. "Shall I tell how I like you best?"

"Stephen," she said in rebuke, flushing, glad it was too dark for him to see her pink cheeks.

He leaned toward her, past the full skirts, and whispered in her ear how he liked her best, then kissed the side of her neck in a long, lingering kiss. Her heart was beating wildly when he finally drew back.

"We are here," he said, with a note of regret plainly in his voice. The carriage had pulled up in front of the brilliantly lit entrance of the squire's huge home, and she had not even noticed that they had stopped.

They heard the laughing and the music as they entered. The squire, red-faced and beaming heartily, met them near the entrance and showed them into the ballroom. Someone took Mary's cloak, and she walked in on Stephen's arm to meet the envious glares and politely jealous smiles of local beauties. It was a proud, strange moment for Mary. How often had she hung over the railing at the Evertons' and watched the guests coming in, wishing she might just stand in the corner for one dance! And here she was, entering on the arm of the most powerful lord in the region, his wife, his possession, in the emerald green dress he had chosen, wearing the family jewels.

Stephen swept her into the dance, a waltz, before she could finish her sad-happy thoughts. He smiled down at her, hugged her quickly when he had the opportunity, released her reluctantly when the squire claimed the honor of a dance with her.

She thought that Stephen would desert her now, and dance with many others. But though he left her for duty dances, he frequently returned to her, merrily cutting out local blades to claim his wife once more. He caused murmurs and frowns and frankly teasing words from many of the men, but he would dance with his Mary, he said.

"Why shouldn't I dance with my wife?" he answered one of the women who dared to rebuke him, though she did it in a merry way. "She is the most beautiful woman here, she dances like a dream, she is as sweet and heady as a Scottish rose. So—" And often he went with her once more, laughing down at her.

She had never enjoyed such a wonderful evening. She felt loved, adored, taken care of, appreciated. He brought her cool champagne to drink, saw to it that her shawl was fetched as they seated themselves near an open French window. He took her in to supper, and carefully filled her plate with the finest delicacies, noting the ones she especially liked.

After supper, the dancing turned more dreamy and sentimental. There were more slow waltzes, and Mary found herself held tightly in the curve of Stephen's arm while he whirled her around and around the huge ballroom. The other dancers were but a blur to her, the figures mere shadows against the background. Nothing was real but the feel of Stephen's arm as it held her, his warm body as he pressed against her momentarily in the dance, as he turned her and swayed with her.

And his voice in her ear, murmuring intimate words, hot words which would have made her blush had she not been so warm already with the dancing and the champagne, dizzy with happiness at being with him.

Nothing happened to mar her pleasure. She kept thinking, this cannot last, it shall end, someone will pull him away from me. It cannot go on, someone will say something cutting, someone will be cruel, someone will wake me to my position, someone will remind me I am but a governess, I do not belong—

But no such thing happened. When she danced with

other men, they were polite, courteous, flattering. She saw little of Christopher; he and Georgiana were deep in their own younger crowd.

Finally the enchanted evening came to an end; their carriage was called, and they said their farewells.

"A lovely evening," she said to Mrs. Demerest.

"Oh, I am so glad you enjoyed it, my lady!" replied the squire's wife, a frown furrowing her brow. "If only the champagne had not run out, and the shrimp was better—and squire said the young people played their games too noisily—"

Mary stared at her. Nothing in the world had gone wrong, she thought. "It was a delightful evening," she said warmly.

They left, and Stephen put his arm about her as soon as they were in the carriage. "Finally alone," he said. "Lord, I thought I would never be alone with you." And he bent down and pressed his lips to the curve of her bare shoulder. "There, that bit has tempted me all evening. And right here—over here—" And he pressed another long, lingering kiss to the hollow of her throat.

She lay back in his arms, the carriage pulling them smoothly away in the darkness, and thought how happy she was with him. When they were completely alone, how radiantly happy she felt!

At the castle, he would not let her go in. They went around to the side, walking in the dampened grass in the moonlit gardens for a time. He held her close, turning her now and then to press her against his warm body, to touch her cheek with his lips, to slide his mouth down the curve of her throat, to hold her, then to walk on again.

They talked, were silent, walked on slowly past the scented roses and phlox. The castle was lighted, but they were alone in the darkness. She heard Christopher laugh, Lady Helena speak crossly to him, then laugh also, Georgiana murmur; then finally the castle was silent.

"We must go in, it is late," said Stephen finally. Over his shoulder, she saw something move; someone was walking in the gardens. She frowned and was about to speak when he added, "Are you too weary, my love? May I come to your bed tonight?"

"Oh—yes, yes, Stephen," she whispered, and came into his arms again. She almost forgot that shadow while they kissed and murmured words of love to each other. Then he took her inside and up to their rooms.

Later, waking, she remembered that figure. Had Christopher been walking alone in the gardens? It had not looked like Christopher; it had not moved like him, lightly and swiftly. It had been dark-cloaked, slow-moving, ominous.

She caught her breath. That figure—it had been coming toward them! Now she remembered that the shadow had been walking toward them as they had turned and hastened to the castle. Stephen had suddenly become impatient and had hurried her teasingly.

But the figure had been following them. A darkly evil figure. Evil seemed to close in on her as she thought of it, and she shivered and drew the blankets up about her shoulders and Stephen's. He was sleeping, and she would not wake him.

How little she really knew of him, she thought, as she tucked the blanket about him. She was not sure of what he was really like. All she knew was that she loved him.

But she could not tell him about the evil that closed in. She could not speak of the shadow that followed. She could not ask him why he had been on the cliffs with the smugglers. She could not question where he went and why he stayed away from her. Or whether he loved her. She knew he desired her body—was that all he wanted from her?

CHAPTER THIRTEEN

MARY SLEPT AGAIN, wakened uneasily. She smelled smoke. In her dreams, half-waking, she imagined herself back in the hunting lodge, with the odor of smoke about her.

Then she wakened abruptly, wide-eyed, sitting up. Stephen was already sliding out of bed. He turned as she roused.

"Mary, I smell smoke!" he said sharply.

"So do I. Where is it coming from?"

He grabbed his robe, slipped it on, and dashed barefoot from the room. She reached for her negligee, put on her slippers, and followed him through her sitting room to the next room, which was his sitting room. Smoke billowed in gray masses from the bedroom where Stephen usually slept.

She cried out and rang for the valet frantically. She pulled and pulled at the bellrope until she heard people coming, running along the hallways, and she opened the door to the hall. She could not see Stephen for the smoke.

"He is in there!" she cried to Wenrick, who arrived first, his gray hair mussed, his flannel nightshirt showing under his heavier robe.

Wenrick was making a dive for the doorway when they both saw Stephen coming out. He was dragging something. As Mrs. Ramsey ran in, they all saw Stephen hauling the body from the room. He laid it down carefully and turned to Mary, the shock plainly on his smoke-grimed face.

"My valet," he said flatly. "Care for him, Mary." And he went back into the room.

The man was lying face down, sprawled limply. Mary went to him, leaned forward to stare incredulously. In the dimly lit room, she saw the knife sticking from his back. The blood about it had already begun to dry.

Mrs. Ramsey knelt beside her, touched the valet's forehead. "Dead an hour or less," she said. "He is still a bit warm." She and Mary stared at each other.

The valet was a quiet, efficient man, who did his work silently, discreetly. He rarely spoke, but Stephen was devoted to him. The man had been with him more than twenty years, Stephen told Mary once. He had gone into the navy with him, served on ships, fought beside him when the pirates attacked. He had nursed Stephen through illness and war wounds.

Now Bonny rushed in, her face more pale than ever. She stared down at the three of them, gave a little incoherent wail of anguish. "No—ah, God—no, no," she finally choked, and began to cry.

Christopher hurried in, his robe slipping from his shoulders, his dark hair mussed. Georgiana followed closely, and then Lady Helena. Lady Helena—Mary stared at her. The woman was as immaculate as ever, rigidly upright in a proper night rail and robe, her hair as smooth as though she had not slept on it. Even that ridiculous blonde bubble remained upright on her forehead.

"What happened? What is it, Mary?" asked Christopher sharply.

"He is dead," said Mary, and then got up. Stephen was still in that bedroom. The others had begun passing buckets of water to each other, slopping the water over the edges of the pails in their haste. They passed them to someone inside—it must be Stephen in there! Stephen—he is still in—I must go—" She tried to rush past Wenrick, but he caught her with unexpected strength and held her back.

"No, my lady! Do not! Stay out here. He will be out soon. The fire is about died out," he said, anxiously, looking toward the smoky interior of the bedroom. She peered past him, trying to find Stephen, seeing only a gray-black figure throwing water on the last flames.

Finally, he came out, his shoulders limp with weariness, his face black with grime. He went right to the valet and knelt beside him, touching him gently.

"Dead. No hope," he said, and his tone was dull and anguished. "Poor fellow. Why, why, would anyone kill him?" He took out the knife slowly, looked at it, laid it aside. Then he turned the valet over.

Mary, standing near Stephen, put her hand to her mouth. The dead eyes were open, seeming to stare up at them. Stephen put his palm over the eyelids and closed them down slowly as though it were a horribly familiar task he had performed often.

Finally he stood up. "We can do nothing tonight," he said, and looked about him as though surprised to see all the people crowded into the sitting room. He looked across thoughtfully at Christopher, at Lady Helena, at the others, as though seeing them for the first time. His eyes were keen and searching behind the red-rimmed eyelids, the black, grimy face. "Evan Basset?" he asked.

Bonny started nervously, muttered, "God help us," and crossed herself. She was staring down at the valet.

"He sleeps in the far wing; he must not have heard the alarm," said Mrs. Ramsey quietly.

Wenrick and Stephen went back into the bedroom to assure themselves that all the flames were thoroughly out. Mary heard them talking in low tones to each other. Mrs.

Ramsey was still kneeling beside the valet, gazing down somberly into his dead face, a little twisted, but peaceful. Bonny stood there shaking, her hands wringing together.

Christopher and Georgiana stood a little closer together. She was crying in fright, and his arm was about her, comforting her. He stared down at the valet, his face oddly thoughtful. Lady Helena stood apart aloofly, glancing about the room, as though the damage from the smoke preoccupied her more than the death of a servant.

"This must be thoroughly aired," she said, half to herself. "And the drapes in the bedroom replaced."

And the valet replaced, Mary thought. But how does one replace an old and trusted servant with whom one has shared so many years? She had seen the look Stephen had given the dead man, one of grief and uncomprehending sorrow. This death had touched him deeply.

Wenrick and the lord of St. John returned, talking like old friends, and Wenrick directed the removal of the body to the crypt in the cellars. The others slowly departed. Mrs. Ramsey paused to offer her help. Mary gently refused it, saying they would talk in the morning.

When they were all gone, Stephen went to Mary's bathroom. His own was smoke-filled, full of grit and splashed with water. He washed thoroughly, put on fresh night-robe, and came back to the bed. But instead of getting in, he sat on the edge, evidently deep in thought.

Mary was far from sleepy, though she was weary. She lay and watched his back for a time, silently. Then she put out her hand and touched his side gently.

"Stephen? It was no accident, was it? It was—murder?"

He nodded and turned about. In the light of the night candle, she saw how drawn and hard he looked. "Yes," he said, dully, without expression. "Murder. A murderer is loose."

"But—who?" she whispered.

"That is what I do not know. What I must discover. Ah,

Mary, I have long dreaded this," he added, strangely, with a heavy sigh. He stretched out, put his long legs under the blankets. "If I had not come to your bed tonight, Mary," he added, quite deliberately, "I believe I should be dead—with a knife—in my chest."

She caught her breath, was silent a moment, then answered. "Yes—I think—so—Stephen. I am afraid so." And she reached out and clutched for his hand with her small cold one.

He enveloped it in a comforting grip. "Ah, now, my Mary, do not fret. We are alive, and I am an old soldier, you know. A salt, and one does not kill a salt easily."

She wanted to say that the valet was an old salt too, and he had been killed. But it had probably not been an easy death. She shuddered, and he felt it and drew her close.

She pretended to sleep, hoping he would relax and sleep also, but she could feel the tension in his body as they lay there. They could not return to slumber peacefully. Death had brushed by them, so close its wings had chilled them.

It seemed that morning would never come. The dawn was gray and cool, cloudy with the threat of rain, and it seemed appropriate to the still heavier mood of the castle.

Mary heard the servants whispering vehemently, and did not rebuke them. She did not have the heart to scold any of them today.

Bonny had come to her that morning to help her wash and dress. The village girl had red-rimmed eyes and heavy lids, as though she had wept instead of sleeping. She was more silent than ever.

Wenrick moved like a tired old man. The footman had no flippant words for the chambermaid. At the breakfast table, Lady Helena sat in silence, her smart blonde head bent over her teacup. She ate nothing, but drank thirstily of the tea.

Mary sat deep in thought, and so, it seemed, were the others.

No, it was not Stephen, she knew that. Stephen would never have killed the man who had served him devotedly for twenty years. They were really close friends, as men were who had fought to the death together. One did not kill for money, not a man like that.

So why? Why had the valet been killed?

Someone had crept into Stephen's room, believing him there, and had found the valet sleeping on the nearby cot. He might have roused the valet, who had fought, struggled—been struck in the back with a long, deadly knife.

The struggle had been evident, even after the fire damage. Tables were overturned, lamps smashed, a rug bloodied.

Someone had crept into Stephen's room believing him there. After the long night of dancing, they had thought he would be too weary to sleep with his wife. They had not counted on his strong sexual urges, thought Mary, with her quick Scottish humor. They had not counted on the urgency between husband and wife, which dancing had increased instead of diminishing.

If Stephen had not come to her—

She shuddered and turned pale. If she had refused him last night, she might be a widow this morning. She looked down across the shining table at Stephen, and thanked God he had come to her last night. It had probably saved his life.

But who, then? She glanced at Lady Helena as the lady motioned the footman to fill her teacup once more. She was distinctively dressed, though pale under the rouge and makeup. But her hair—it was smart and swept up so high, just like last night.

The bubble-blonde hair just as at the ball. As though she had not slept on it.

As though she might have paced the floor.

Or walked through hallways to the bedroom of the man who stood between her son and a vastly rich inheritance!

"Eat, Mother, you have eaten nothing today," said Christopher suddenly. Lady Helena started, and the teacup shook in her slim hand. She stared across at her son, tried to smile, but the hard mouth trembled.

"Yes, do Mother. It has been a shock, but we must bear up. I am going to talk to Daddy," said Georgiana with unexpected determination. "He must know of this."

Stephen stirred in his chair. "I am going to speak with him today. Christopher, I wish you would come with us. It must be reported, and I will need a further witness."

"Yes, sir," said Christopher with unusual meekness. He stared down at his plate, where the food was scarcely more touched than was his mother's.

Lady Helena gazed across at him fondly, affection stirring in her eyes. "Don't go if it will upset you, darling," she said. "It is Stephen's business, he will take care of it."

"I must help also, Mother," he said, and smiled at her. "Father would have done the same, I am sure. We must find the bastard who did that horrible thing."

Lady Helena did not even rebuke his language. She merely nodded her smart gray-blonde head. "You are very like your father," she said, with a little sigh. "So much like him, darling. Sometimes when I look at you, I see your father all over again. Now, Stephen is more like his mother." And discontent crept into her voice. "She was as dark as a Spaniard."

A slight gleam of amusement came into Stephen's sherry-brown eyes. Mary recalled the portrait of his father and thought, no, Lady Helena is wrong. Stephen is more like his father than his mother, and Christopher is more like his mother. But Lady Helena chose to think Christopher was like his dear departed father, who had spoiled and indulged her crazily.

Was this the answer? Suddenly Mary was alert, and let the suggestions fill her mind, analyzing them carefully. Lady Helena adored her only son; she thought nothing was too good for him. She wanted the world for him—but he was only the younger half brother of the Lord of St. John. However, if Stephen died—without heirs—the castle and lands would all go to Christopher.

He would then be Lord of St. John.

Did Lady Helena want this enough to kill for him? Would her obsession, her possessive love for her son, go this far? She clung to Stephen a little, depending on him for support. But to Christopher she gave all her domineering, devouring love. She had even chosen his wife for him, a meek girl she could command.

Would Lady Helena kill for her son?

A footman came in, bent and murmured to Stephen. Mary caught some of the words, "Mr. Basset—later—study—"

Stephen nodded, his face turning grim and hard. "I will see him at nine thirty," he said curtly.

And Mary remembered the scene in the sitting room, and Bonny's horrified face. What did the village girl know? Was it connected with the village, with the smugglers?

It was not just important to find out how the valet had died, and at whose hand.

It was vitally important to find out *why* the man had died.

Where could she go and look for an answer? Mary sat and pondered a long time. Her tea grew cold; the food went uneaten. Stephen left the table. He paused beside her to kiss her cool cheek, to say he would see her in his study at ten. She nodded.

"And eat something, my darling. You must keep up

your strength," he added very gently, and touched her cheek with his long, strong fingers.

She nodded again and tried to smile. After he had left the room, Lady Helena spoke sharply. "My lady, are you ill? I have been wondering if you are ill." And her eyes went obviously to Mary's bosom and waist.

Mary felt herself flushing hotly, especially as Christopher and Georgiana stared at her also. Not wanting her to have an heir. Not wanting her to interfere with their plans for their future.

"No, not ill, I thank you, Lady Helena," she said gently. "Only feeling the strain of last night—as we all do, I am sure." She let the footman fill her cup with fresh tea, then motioned him to Lady Helena.

The lady let her cup be filled, and she drank again. Georgiana was stirring restlessly, waiting for the others to be finished. Mary finally ate a few bites, then indicated they might leave the table.

She herself retreated to a small sitting room, where she often consulted with Mrs. Ramsey. She wanted to get her thoughts in order before she talked to Stephen.

But what could she say? How could she confess now that she had seen him on the cliffs with the smugglers? How could she ask him if the murder of the valet was connected with Stephen's activities with the smugglers?

She could not.

She sat with her hands folded on her lap. She wore a white muslin gown with green ribbons. There were diamonds on her fingers, a fine emerald on her hand. She wore a diamond brooch, fine shoes, silk next to her skin.

And she was miserable, because she did not know what to believe.

Her husband might be a murderer, the leader of a vicious smuggling ring. And his valet might have been killed to silence him, or to get at Stephen. Many people around might be full of revenge against Stephen.

How could she protect him? Could she, should she protect him, if he had murdered? If the attack last night had been revenge against his own murdering?

She put her face in her hands and moaned aloud. She knew no answers, no answers at all.

CHAPTER FOURTEEN

TEN O'CLOCK CAME all too soon, and Mary walked along the long corridor of family portraits back to her husband's study. She wanted to pause at each one and study the face, and trace some resemblance to her husband, but she knew she was evading the moment when she must talk to Stephen.

Some strange feeling had come over her, some intuition born of her keen Scottish mind and her emotions. Something was going to happen.

As she approached the half-open door, she heard voices raised in argument. She paused, winced, then went on apprehensively. As she stepped in the door, she saw Stephen standing behind his desk facing Christopher. Both were flushed, staring at each other, seemingly equally determined.

"But this is insane!" Christopher was storming, one fist raised in protest. "To move with our goods tomorrow—"

"Some cases only. There are linens and supplies at the manor house," said Stephen. "You will do as I say! I have told you about this before; you could have prepared your wife for it! I always mean what I say!"

"But it was only a week ago that you suggested we live there!" shouted Christopher, in his frustration, pounding the desk. "You said that sometime we might be interested in moving there and using it as our residence! You offered me the title of viscount that went with it! But we are comfortable here! Georgiana is not yet prepared to run a house, she needs—"

"You will have Lady Helena with you. She can assist your wife in the management until Georgiana is prepared to assume all her duties." The tone had turned cold and inflexible. Stephen turned his head sharply as Mary came in, but his gaze did not soften. He looked at her as frigidly as he was surveying his half brother. "Ah, Mary, come in. I was asking Christopher to be ready to move on the morrow."

She stared at him, then at Christopher. "To—morrow?" she asked blankly. "But surely, Stephen, it is asking a lot—"

And she felt as bewildered as Christopher looked. The younger man stormed out of the room, probably to consult his wife and mother. She walked slowly over to the desk and looked at Stephen. He avoided her gaze and sat down slowly and heavily. "The manor house is in sad condition," he said, rather sullenly, staring down at the papers before him. "When I surveyed it last week, I was shocked. The lands have been allowed to fall into ruin. I want him to remove at once to Penhurst and take up occupancy."

She bit her lip on a protest. In Stephen's present somber mood, it was futile to protest about anything. She felt completely bewildered. Penhurst was a day's journey by fast horse. It would take Christopher and his mother and wife almost two days by coach. And to pack and go on the morrow— She sat down slowly across from Stephen, folded her hands, and waited.

He finally looked up, but stared beyond her rather than at her. "If you will assist them in moving, I should be grateful, Mary," he said, with quiet, deadly control. He looked as she might imagine he would look as he ordered his ship made ready for a battle.

"Of course, Stephen," she said gently. "I will request Mrs. Ramsey's assistance. They will take only their clothing and a few possessions now, I presume?"

He seemed relieved at her understanding. "Yes, that is correct. There is no need to pack household items. All is at Penhurst. It is well furnished," he added, and reached for some papers. He handed them to her. She had time to think that he had said the place was in sad condition, and now he said they would have excellent supplies! He was not consistent, and this alone told of an upheavel of his spirits, for he was usually a very logical man.

She looked over the papers because they gave her hands and her eyes something to do. They listed the inventories of the house and grounds at Penhurst, and sounded formidable. They also did not give the impression of the decrepit condition which Stephen had decided made their visit urgent.

"Will—Christopher—and the others—stay for some time?" she asked with seeming casualness, turning over a page of kitchen items.

"That depends on how quickly things can be arranged. However, if they return here soon, I should expect it to be only for a short visit. This will be their permanent home, as I have intended all along. The principle under which I operate," and here a note of humor crept into his tone, "is that no house is big enough for more than one mistress. And you are mistress here, not Lady Helena."

Mary looked up quickly, her head coming up with a toss of red curls, to find he was smiling slightly, the familiar smile which relaxed his mouth and made it less stern. His sherry-brown eyes shared the joke with her and made her understand that he knew what difficulties she had had with Lady Helena.

"Thank you, Stephen," she said, rather shyly, coloring. "But I—I do not understand this haste—surely it can wait a few days or a week, even a month. They should have time to pack—"

"What I say exactly," said Lady Helena's sharp, angry tone, as she bustled into the room. She was followed more slowly by Christopher and Georgiana. "Why the haste, Stephen? You seem anxious to be rid of us! I cannot comprehend—"

A sharp argument followed in which Stephen allowed his usual smooth courtesy to drop and spoke some rude words which Mary thought should never have been uttered. Lady Helena was deeply offended, and really hurt under her sophisticated exterior. Mary caught the flash of the blue eyes, the puzzled grief as they rested on her stepson. He had always treated her with great courtesy and deference. What had come over him? And Lady Helena bluntly and angrily asked that question before they retired from his study.

The housekeeper was summoned, and she and maids and footmen set to work packing. The other three were rushing about, too bewildered to help, and managed only to get in the way. The dinner that evening was so strained that Mary was thankful to have it over. No one remained for coffee; Stephen rushed back to his study to shut himself in, the others went to their rooms to supervise more packing.

The next morning they were on their way. Evan Basset had come to see them off, and he and Lady Helena held a long, low-toned conversation before Lady Helena stepped into the coach.

Stephen was grim, aloof. Lady Helena looked as though she would burst into tears, as did Georgiana, and Christopher was obviously confused.

After the coaches had departed, rumbling down the long avenue, Mary went to the jade sitting room to think. She had another cup of tea, but it did little to clear away the cobwebs which seemed to have formed so thickly about her brain.

What was wrong with Stephen? Why had he done this? He was so fond of Christopher that he had spoiled him outrageously. He liked Georgiana, and patted her on the head as though she were little more than a child. He had deferred to Lady Helena, seemed fond of her, rarely rebuked her, rarely criticized her, even when his own wife was attacked.

Why had he sent them away? For that was really what had happened, she thought.

She began to shiver, and realized it was with fear. She was afraid of Stephen. He was behaving so oddly, and she could not put from her mind the memory of him striding up the cliff path in the night, up from the smugglers' ships. Was this all connected with his activities? Had someone discovered him to be the smuggler?

Or—she shuddered convulsively and leaned forward to hold out her hands to the fire—had he seen her on the cliffs? Was that it? Had he decided that, much as he adored her body, he must be rid of this potential threat to his activities? Would he—

Oh, dear God in heaven, thought Mary. Was he insane? Would he murder her? Had he sent them away—out of the way—not to be witnesses?

Did he mean to kill her quietly?

She sat shivering and staring into the fire. Finally, cold and stiff and rent with fears, she made herself stand up. Her hands twisted together in an agony of indecision. To whom could she turn? The squire? Would he believe her? A practical, dogmatic man who believed only what he saw under his nose? No.

The vicar? A meek, mild man afraid of his shadow? No.

No village man would dare offend the lord, no matter

how independent he felt in his own domain. Not even the innkeeper.

Evan Basset. She thought of him with sudden immense relief. He was so calm, so competent. And he had known the family for many years.

She did not pause to do more than throw a scarf over her shoulders. She half-ran through the long halls and corridors, through the main great hall, down the other wing, toward Evan Basset's rooms. She knocked urgently at the great wooden doors.

Evan Basset himself opened the door to her, took her cold hand in his, and drew her in. His face was somber. "My lady Mary," he said quietly. "Come in. Come to the fire."

She went over to it and put her hands to the warm blaze. She was shuddering again, in spite of the thick shawl. "Mr. Basset," she said urgently, "I will not disturb you long."

"It is your husband and his actions," he said quietly. He nodded his graying head slowly. "Yes, I have seen it coming on."

Mary stared at him, her lips parted, her great green eyes questioning. "Is he—is he—insane?" she finally brought out the horrible question.

He did not answer this. His lips compressed tightly, his brows drew together in a frown. "You had best leave this castle," he finally said, after a long pause. His tone was heavy, weary.

"Leave? I, leave? Why did he send the others away?"

"I do not know, Lady Mary. But you are lovely and young, as young as—Angela," he said, and his thoughts were so like hers that she shook with fear. Angela—bloody and murdered— "You must leave. It is not safe for you here. Leave. Leave tonight. Leave now!"

"What? How can—but answer my questions! Is he insane? Why did he send Christopher away from him! He loves the boy! He has spoiled him—"

"So did his father," said Evan Basset. He went over to a table, and opened the drawer. He took out a weighted velvet bag.

He came over to her and placed the small, heavy bag in her hand. "Here is money, more than enough for a time. Go to London; take your maid with you. Settle there in some respectable place. I will send you more money, as much as you shall require. Leave him."

"Leave—Stephen?" The money burned her hand, but she could not drop it. She stared at him blankly, unable to read his expression. The lids were hooded, heavy over the weary eyes.

"Leave him. Get a divorce. You can get one in London. But most urgently—leave today. Get your maid to pack a few necessary items and leave! I will order the horses brought around; there is another comfortable traveling coach you may use. I will have all ready in two hours, I promise you!"

It was too much, too suddenly. She shook her head. "No, no, you can't mean it! You can't mean I should leave Stephen, divorce him! Why—no one divorces!"

"If the situation is desperate, it is possible," he said with cold significance. "If you remain—you may not live, Lady Mary! Go, go while you still live, while your young, fresh face is still mobile with expression, and your eyes can move—"

She shuddered violently and cried out. He put his hand gently on her shoulder, turned her toward the door. "Go," he said, urgently. "Go! I will have the coach ready in two hours! Go!"

She left him dazed, more bewildered than when she had come. She had hoped for calm reasoning, a laughing away of her fears, a logical explanation of Stephen's behavior, perhaps a rational, boring lecture on the poor state of the

Penhurst estate. Instead—this command to go, divorce Stephen, take the money and get out in two hours! It was not reasonable!

Her temper was rising; she knew it because she had stopped shivering and was ready to fling off the shawl. She felt hot with temper and fury. What was going on? She would find out! She would, though they struck her, though Stephen struck her, she would know!

She marched to Stephen's study, finding the door closed. She flung it open and faced him across the wide room. Her eyes widened when she saw that on the pile of papers on his desk there lay a large hand pistol! It was black and gleaming, the handle a duller shade, showing signs of use. It was his navy pistol. He moved his hand slowly toward another pile of papers, as though it had been moving toward the pistol.

"Well, Mary?" He did not stand; his tone was curt. She studied the cold sherry-brown eyes.

"Sir, I would like a good and a true and a satisfying explanation of your actions! I went to Evan Basset, and rather than explain to me, he advised me to go to London! He gave me this, told me to divorce you! Sir, I wish to know—"

He stood up slowly and went around to her. Involuntarily, she shrank from him, then stood stiffly as he took the velvet pouch from her. He opened it, stirred the money with his finger, closed it again. "It is enough for now," he said. "Though you may take more with you. Take Bonny, she is a good, sensible girl." He dropped the pouch in her nerveless hand.

She stared up at him. "Sir, I am asking you if you are insane!" she said, quite clearly, outraged and furious. Her eyes flashed at him. "Are you mad? What is the reason behind all this? Why did you send Christopher away? There is no need to send him so quickly—"

"Perhaps I am jealous of him," said Stephen, not smiling.

His sherry-brown eyes gleamed. "There is no need to explain anything to you, Mary. You will do as I order you! Go to London, await me there. I will come when I can. Or if I do not come, do as—as Evan Basset commands. Get a divorce, forget me. The attorneys will see to you. I have written out their address. Here it is." And he placed a piece of paper in her hand.

She stared at it, at him, her mind going blank. He wanted her to leave? He wanted her to divorce him? Was he truly insane? Or was he tired of her at last?

"But—but Stephen," she said, the fire in her dying abruptly. She felt desolate, lost. She had felt so warm in his arms, so loved, so adored. Now—suddenly—to know she had lost him was pain so appalling she could think of nothing else. She whispered, "Are you—tired of me—already?"

"You may well think so," he said curtly, and turned back to his papers. "Did Basset say anything about a coach for you?"

She could not answer. Blindly, she turned to the door and rushed out. He did not call her back. She stumbled along the same hallway through which she had just marched with Scottish head high. She wanted to weep, but could not. She was too stunned.

She went up to her suite and stood looking about the rooms where she had known a happiness as she had never experienced before in her hard-working life. Such nights in his arms, such days dreaming of him. Light banter with him, flowers brought in from him, gifts, adoring looks—All this ended. She stood with her eyes closed and felt a knife twisting in her heart. She put her hand slowly to her breast and pressed it, but could not ease the heaviness there.

Stephen, she thought. Stephen. And could not say his name aloud. She loved him, but he was weary of her already. He had said so. Weary of her—through. Finished.

It was over. The dream was ended, the fragile, questing dream which had scarcely formed like a little bubble of shimmering iridescence in the summer air. Gone.

She thought of the long, jagged scar on his left cheek, and wished she had kissed it once more the last night he had spent with her. She thought of him in bed with her, and it was agony for her to remember. He had been wearying of her even then, even as he held her and kissed her and whispered warm, hungry words. She twisted the rings on her left hand and found them too tight to remove. How could she bear to remove the rings he had put on her? She could not, any more than she could remove the chains he had put on her body, her soul, her mind.

She belonged to him utterly—but he did not want her anymore. She loved him completely, adored him—but he did not want that love and adoration.

"My lady?" It was Bonny's whisper. Mary turned around slowly, painfully. She felt as stiff as she had the night she had lain out on the cliffs and witnessed the smugglers. Stiff and sore and cold and wounded to the heart.

Wounded unto death. What use to go? What if he killed her with a knife? He had already done her to death, she thought.

"I am to pack for you, my lady," said Bonny, and her lip quivered. "I am to go—with you—to London." And she made it sound like a sentence to prison.

"Yes, Bonny. Take only a few practical clothes," said Mary, and was astounded at the calmness of her tone. "You will also pack a trunk for yourself. The coach will be ready soon. Have the footmen bring three trunks to the rooms here."

Bonny packed in silence. Mary blessed her for her common sense. She packed a few jewels, her mother's brooch, the few treasures that Stephen had given her personally for her to keep, none of the family treasures. She would take only what might belong to herself alone. And what matter? Did a corpse need to dress for dinner? Would a dead body look better in an emerald necklace?

Mad thought flitted through her brain, even as she calmly ordered the footmen and Bonny and Mrs. Ramsey. The good housekeeper was plainly flustered and disturbed by all the moving, and hovered anxiously about, not her usual, efficient self.

Stephen was not even there to bid them good-bye. He merely sent another packet of money by the butler and bade her to see the solicitors soon as she reached London! Mary stared at the butler who gave her this incongruous practical advice, shook her red head, and stepped into the coach. She kept peering back, but Stephen did not even appear at a window, as far as she could tell.

Bonny was silent, only wiping at her eyes with a clean white handkerchief, silently crying, silently grieving for herself and her mistress. The coachman was silent, not even cursing the horses, and the footman who had been sent with them, one of the older men, was as quiet as a tomb. She wondered briefly how they had all been ready to depart so rapidly.

They avoided the village and turned directly into the highway to one side of it. Mary watched the familiar scenery turning into the more distant unfamiliar, and felt a pain such as she had never known, even at the death of her parents. She was leaving Stephen, the coach was taking her rapidly away from him. It could not be—it was impossible—

Impossible.

Her mind began to function after hours of seeming blankness. She shook her head sharply. Her hands were idle in her lap; she removed her gloves and twisted the rings again slowly. Think, think, Mary, she urged herself. Ye are weary, ye are hurt, but *think*. What is wrong? What pieces are missing?

Why had Stephen acted like this? Why had Evan Basset urged her to leave? Why, why, why? What possible reason?

And why, she scolded herself, are ye on the road to London while your heart remains behind with him? Why are ye running away at the first word he speaks sharply to you? Are ye not used to difficulties?

And who ever solved a problem by running from it?

She could hear her father speak those very words. "How can ye solve a problem, Mary mine, by running from it? No, face up to the problem, think, Mary, think, and solve it!"

They had been on the journey almost two hours. Why, why was she going so meekly to London? Repeatedly she asked herself the question but could not find an answer.

Bonny sobbed, put her handkerchief to her mouth, and muttered an apology. Mary nodded absently, glancing toward the girl. Bonny had much common sense, and she saw no reason for this either.

Why was she weakly doing what was commanded? Why did she not use her own God-given brains and figure out an answer for herself? She tightened her lips. The hurt was dulling. The strangeness of it all was striking her more and more completely.

No, Stephen had not acted like himself. He was usually commanding and hard and expected his orders to be carried out. Yet—he was kind to his stepmother, adoring of his brother, devoted to Mary once he had come to her. Then—why the sudden change? All in one day! As soon as the valet was murdered!

Mary frowned. She was going in the wrong direction to solve any mysteries. She reached up and tapped sharply on the roof of the coach.

The horses pulled up. The footman got down and came about to the window. "Yes, my lady? Do you wish something?" he asked anxiously.

"Yes, Groves. Tell Foster to turn about. We are going back," she said calmly.

The footman stared at her. She heard Bonny's caught breath.

"Going—back—my lady?" he asked slowly. "But my lord said that we should convey you to London with all speed."

"I said we shall go back, and go back we shall. With all speed," she said ironically, and leaned back and closed her eyes.

The footman gave the message to the coachman. The horses were turned about, and they headed back toward the Castle of St. John. Mary felt an immense relief. They were going back. She might have to leave again, but she would not leave without a damn good reason, she said strongly to herself.

Stephen would have to talk to her. He would have to convince her he was right in this. She would have to know for certain that he was discarding her—before she would accept dismissal.

After all, she had been a governess, she thought, with a flash of Scottish humor. She would not have accepted dismissal from her governess post without reason! Nor would she accept dismissal from her duties as wife of a lord—not without adequate cause!

She sat quietly, hiding her rising anxiety and impatience as the horses trotted back to the stables of the castle. They knew they were on their way home, too, she thought.

Home. Home. His home was her home, and it would never be any different.

The two hours seemed endless, but finally, leaning from the window, she saw the towers of the Castle of St. John; never had they looked so inviting to her. The horses broke into a faster trot as they climbed up the winding hill. Finally they were at the foot of the long staircase leading up into the castle.

Mary jumped out with the help of the footman. She picked up her skirts and fairly flew up the long stairs, not waiting for Bonny. The door was open and she went inside, standing in the large entrance hall looking about. Where was Wenrick? Where was the footman on duty! Both gone.

She looked about with growing bewilderment. No one was in sight. It was as though an evil spirit had waved a wand and caused everyone to vanish! She could not find Stephen, not in his study or any of the drawing rooms. His papers were in a neat pile on the desk, no sign of disturbance. Mrs. Ramsey had disappeared; no servant came in answer to her impatient calling.

She returned to the doorway, and saw that the coach, Bonny, and the two men were gone. She felt an uneasy twinge of fear. How could everyone disappear so rapidly? It was chilling.

She panicked. She picked up her skirts again, and ran through the huge echoing old castle, down the long corridors and into the wing where Evan Basset lived. She had some idea vaguely in her mind that if disaster had struck the rest of the castle, she would be safe there.

She pounded on the huge wooden doors. After a long, heartrending pause, they slowly opened. To her relief, Evan Basset was there, smiling down at her, looking so normal and natural in his outdoor clothes that she could not refrain from smiling back at him and saying impulsively, "How good to find you here! I was quite frightened! No one seems to be about—"

"I heard you had returned, Lady Mary," he said, quite calmly. "Come in, come in. Let me make you comfortable, and I will order some tea. You have had a chilly journey —and all for nothing."

"Thank you," she said a little blankly at this welcome. He opened another door for her, and then suddenly shoved her quickly inside, and closed and locked the door after her!

She turned about, calling, but heard him laugh outside the door. "Evan!" she cried. "Mr. Basset—what is this, sir? What are you—"

Then she saw him. Her husband. Stephen, lying on the floor, his face and head quite bloody. Lying limply, seeming to be dead. Like the valet. Only his eyes were closed. She screamed and dropped on her knees at his side.

"Stephen, Stephen," she moaned, and felt for him blindly, feeling his face and head frantically. He felt warm, not cold. Was he recently dead?

"Oh, my God, my God, help me, help me, my God—" She touched the throat timidly, hopefully. Yes, there was a pulse—a strong, hard pulse.

Alive. But like this—his head bloody— She moaned, and lifted him up a little, cradling him against her thankfully. He was alive. Alive. But why were they locked in here? What had happened to him? She thought she would go mad if there were no explanation for all this.

CHAPTER FIFTEEN

STEPHEN SEEMED to be breathing more easily. Mary carefully laid him down again on the rug and looked about. They were locked in a bedroom, an elaborate room with French rug, velvet drapes, a huge canopied bed of gold. She grimaced. She went to the bathroom, wrung out several cold cloths, and returned to Stephen.

She bent over him, finally sat down on the rug, and gently lifted him into her lap, bathing his head. She murmured to him lovingly. "Stephen, Stephen, darling? Are you awake? Love—are you awake? Stephen?"

Finally, he opened his eyes and stared up at her. A puzzled frown creased his dark brows as he gazed. Then his eyes cleared and shone. "Mary, is that you?"

"Yes, Stephen. Do you remember what happened?"

"You left me," he said dreamily, not like his usual curt self. "The coach—rolled away—down the avenue—"

"I came back," she said gently. "I was not satisfied with you. I had to talk to you, had to find answers—"

"My Mary," he muttered, and she bent and put her cheek next to his.

She felt him tense. He moved, put his hand to his head.

"Evan Basset," he muttered. He looked about him, sat up slowly, and cursed. "Damn that Evan. Bastard. I came to confront him—I suspected—"

"Suspected what, Stephen?" she asked. "He has locked us in here. Where are all the servants?"

"I sent them away also. Out of danger. I had come to suspect Basset. He is head of the smugglers, I fear, Mary, and also behind the murders. I wanted to confront him without danger to anyone else—"

"So you sent us all away." An immense relief filled her heart even as she worried about Basset. As he winced, she asked quickly, "Your head—Stephen—did he injure you—"

"He struck me from behind. Fool trick, and I fell for it. I turned, and he struck me—I remember now." He lifted his hand to his head. "I'm all right. We must talk with him, he is a reasonable man—"

She bit her lips. Evan Basset was not acting like a reasonable man. How could a murderer be a reasonable man? She watched in silence as Stephen rubbed another cold cloth across his face. There was a heavy gash in his forehead which bled anew.

She stood up as Stephen felt carefully at the back of his head. "Let me see that," she said, and inspected the wound carefully. "It is bad, Stephen," she told him quietly. "It is bleeding, and the cut is open an inch or more. Let me—"

"No, not now." He pushed her away firmly. "I must speak to Basset. We must get this matter settled. Of course, he will have to leave." He sighed heavily. "Father trusted him too much, I fear. When I returned from the wars, I trusted him at first. Then little things began to add up. The people feared us both, yet they scarcely knew me. I had to find out why they feared. No one would talk to me about it. Even our servants here were wary, the ones who had lived here a long time."

"He has had his own way for years. He must have felt that he owned or controlled the land," said Mary slowly, her eyes alert. And I doubted Stephen also, she thought. I saw him on the cliffs and immediately concluded that he was head of the smuggling ring. And it must have been Evan Basset all the time.

"I must know," said Stephen, and just then the door unlocked with a click and was opened. Evan Basset stood there, a heavy pistol weighing down his right hand.

He looked at them and smiled his usual pleasant, calm smile. "Well, you are up and talking. Come with me. I must make an end of all this, you see."

Mary caught her breath sharply. He was insane. He must be, standing there as calmly as ever, with that deadly pistol in his hand, his eyes glittering. She put her hand on Stephen's arm to quiet him as he would have stepped forward.

"I must say we are curious about you, Mr. Basset," she said, as calmly as Evan. She felt Stephen's arm hard under her fingers, and she pressed her fingers tightly about the arm. "Would you answer but a few questions for us? Not that it would take up much of your time!"

He shrugged. "There is plenty of time, my dear Lady Mary. I do regret the necessity of killing you. I was sending you to London to get you out of the way; you really should have gone and waited for me."

"Waited for you, sir?" she asked, her eyes wide. "Would you have come for me, then?"

"You are an arrogant bastard!" Stephen burst out furiously. "How dare you think you could take over my land, my wife—"

"Oh, yes," said Evan Basset, rather dreamily, standing there in the doorway, pistol in hand, eyes shining. "I have planned it for years. I will get rid of you, my Lord Stephen! You are too much in my way. You should have stayed in London and let me run affairs down here, as I did for your late father! He never interfered with me."

"And I—I remained in London—gambled, and you never rebuked me," said Stephen, slowly, consideringly. "I returned from the wars, disillusioned, bitter, angry, ready to raise hell. And you encouraged me. Yes, you wanted me to be a rake, an idler, while you did as you pleased here. And when I came down to the country, there were always parties, gaming, ladies, to distract me. And Angela—"

"Yes, Angela. She was smarter than you, I fear. Those beautiful eyes saw too much, and I had to get rid of her. Sadly. I killed her sadly, I assure you. And your dog Commander. He was sniffing about and trying to bark. Bad as Angela, sniffing about, trying to learn what was going on."

"So—you killed Angela," said Mary hastily, feeling the tension mounting in Stephen's arm. He was becoming so enraged, she feared he would do something foolish and untimed. "And the valet, you killed him also?"

"Yes, I really meant to kill Stephen, but he was sleeping with his seductive wife. You really messed things up for me, Lady Mary! Your eyes are too sharp for your own good. And you did go down to the cliffs and see the smugglers, didn't you? One of my agents thought he saw you returning that morning."

"Yes, I saw the men—the smugglers. But not you, Evan Basset," she said, "and I did not suspect you—until just now."

Stephen was growling low in his throat with his rage. Mary kept a tight grip on his arm.

"So you meant to kill Stephen and killed the valet instead. And you had killed Angela—to prevent her finding out and telling Stephen. And the dog. And what did you mean to do with the rest of us?" she asked, as though calmly curious. She really did want to know. It fascinated her, the planning of this insane man.

"Oh, I planned to kill Christopher, but Lord Stephen sent him away. I shall manage when they come here for your funeral. They shall all meet with an unfortunate accident in their coach, I believe." And he actually smiled. "I shall kill you and set fire to some room—ah, your bedrooms, I believe. Yes, that will do nicely. There will be nothing left of your bodies, and it will be very sad. I think I shall weep at your funeral. Then Christopher will meet with his unfortunate accident, and his wife and Lady Helena shall die with him. And I shall be left with the management of the estate, and no one to inherit. The title will be unclear for years, and I shall take and squirrel away whatever I wish."

And he laughed softly, as though his plans pleased him immensely.

Stephen said, almost gently, "And the smuggling. Why, when you had so much money, the family jewels, the paintings—all this wealth? Why the smuggling also, Evan Basset? Are you so greedy?"

Basset frowned. "Greedy? Ah, no. I have been doing this for years, all through the late war. Napoleon was anxious for English gold. And there is a lively market for tea and brandy and tobacco. It continues, you know. The markets are quite good. And you—my Lord Stephen, you thought yourself so grand and commanding when you had a hundred or so men to rule! I have more than that! More than two hundred men under me, who do instantly whatever I say! And the countryside in my grip—" And he held out his left hand proudly, then crushed it closed. "And they dare not defy me! Or murder is their punishment!"

His eyes glittered insanely. Mary shuddered and shrank back against Stephen. Her husband put her gently from him, and she felt him bracing himself. He kept on talking to Evan Basset.

"I can understand then. You wanted power as well as wealth. That is reasonable, yes, I see that. And you took the jewels from Father's room, and the vaults. That was why I could never find them. You said father had pawned them. I searched, and had my agents search the markets here and abroad, and found no trace of them. That was when I began to suspect you."

"I thought you did. *My* agents reported you were searching!" And Basset turned his head and laughed at Mary, who was staring at him, wide-eyed. "Oh, my dear Lady Mary," he said mockingly. "You believed whatever I said! How you swallowed my—"

Stephen sprang at him, and caught him off guard. The two men struggled over the pistol, and it went off with a deafening roar. Basset dropped the empty pistol and fought with Stephen, showing wiry strength Mary had not known he possessed.

She jumped back, watched with her heart in her mouth as they fought. Stephen's face was grimly set, the blood trickling down over his forehead at the strain. Then Basset managed to get the knife from his belt.

"No—no—look out, Stephen—," cried Mary—but too late.

The knife stabbed home, right into Stephen's shoulder. Stephen was turning; it caught him in the flesh above the bone, and he groaned, and staggered back, holding his shoulder. Basset grabbed the pistol from the floor and reloaded it, watching Stephen with a scowl.

Stephen started for him again, though the knife stuck from the wound. Basset grabbed Mary and held her in front of him, the pistol to her temple.

"One step and I kill her," he said, with a growl of rage.

Stephen paused. Then in a very calm tone he said, "Well, Basset. I'll take out this knife carefully and drop it on the floor. It is sticking me."

"Little I care for that," said Basset, but watched him alertly as Stephen carefully pulled out the knife and dropped it on the floor. Blood gushed from the wound, past the torn velvet of Stephen's red coat.

"You have angered me," said Evan Basset, in a deadly, strange tone. His voice was higher pitched, odd. "I shall not kill you quietly, I think. Why should I make it easy for you? What shall I do with you? Ah—yes, I know. This way."

He nodded toward the door. "What then?" asked Stephen, not moving.

"Go as I bid you!" Evan pushed the point of the pistol so strongly at Mary's head that she flinched. His other hand held her in such a tight grip that her arm seemed to be numb. "Go ahead of us, slowly! Do as I tell you! I do the commanding here!"

Stephen gave Mary's face a long look, then he nodded, and turned, and walked ahead of them. Evan Basset shoved Mary and she followed Stephen, still held tightly in Basset's grip. They walked through the luxuriously furnished apartments. She saw Stephen give long, recognizing stares at the portraits, the jewels in the glass case, books, porcelain, ivory.

"So this is where they all went," said Stephen quietly. "It is interesting to have the mystery solved."

"You will not live long, just long enough. You may think of this as you die!" jeered Basset, behind Mary. Mary wondered what he meant. How did he mean to kill them?

He pushed them toward the back stairs. Stephen opened doors slowly on command, paused on the stairway until they joined him. They heard voices as they walked down the narrow stone stairs, and came into the cellars beneath the castle.

Voices came more clearly to them, arguing voices, quarreling tones, and the sounds of heavy kegs being thumped about.

They came through one huge barrel vault into another room and paused. Ahead of them Mary saw two rooms full of men, and kegs, and packets, and bundles. Faces —faces of men from the farms, and village, and Jeremiah Shaw!

They stared at each other across the men. Jeremiah's face was blank. He was lifting a huge keg, and he put it down deliberately on the shelf behind him, then turned back and folded his arms. He was with them, one of the smugglers, she thought, with a pang. Or—was he? His look was strange and warning to her.

"Look at my new prizes," said Evan Basset's strong voice behind her. He shoved her forward roughly, unexpectedly, so she fell forward and onto the stone floor. She fell heavily and sprawled there. Stephen started, but was halted by Basset's voice. "Let her be! Men, look at what I have. The lord of the castle, lord of you, and he is in my power! What shall I do with him? Tell me how to kill him. You shall have a rare show!"

The murmuring had stopped. There was a dead silence for a long moment as the men stared from one to the other of them. Mary lifted herself up painfully, then crawled to the side of the room, hoping she was out of Basset's range of vision. She found herself at the feet of several rough farm men, their heavy boots near her head. Behind her were shelves set out for the kegs of brandy. Tall shelves. She lifted herself cautiously up to sit on the first one.

"Well—tell me—how shall they die? They are the enemy, they would stop our smuggling! They are poking and prying about," said Basset, impatiently, lifting his pistol carelessly and waving it at them. Mary noted that the men winced from his threat and avoided his gaze. They were all afraid of him, all but Jeremiah Shaw, who stared steadily back at Basset.

Finally one of the men called out with a rough laugh, "Torture, Basset. How about torture?" There was muttering among them, frowns, some called out, "Yea, yea. Torture and death! Too good for them, a-messing in our business!"

"Yes, torture," said Basset, satisfied, his eyes glittering madly. "I shall let you take turns with the irons and the pokers! Stir up the fire! Let them scream first! I enjoy the screaming! Let the aristocrats who live on us have a taste of what we get when we disobey them! Do you remember the riots when you were children? Burn them! Burn them!"

Stephen spoke up sharply. "Did my father treat you cruelly? The only bad thing he ever did to you was to put this man in charge! That was wickedly foolish! But did my father ever mistreat you? And as for me—I fought for you against the French! I fought on decks with you men, some of you fought with us! We beat off the French—while he profited by our wounds!"

"Aye, aye, that he did—," one man muttered, and was silenced by the man beside him.

Mary stared up at her husband. She thought he had never looked so grand, though his velvet jacket was torn, his face bloody, his hands grimy. His eyes shone with fervor as he pleaded with them. "We have fought together, lads! Fight with me once again! Fight against this new tyrant who would enslave you, who has held you in iron grip and tormented your bodies and your souls! He has threatened your wives and your children! Has murdered your friends! How long will you live thus?"

Basset struck at him. Stephen stepped swiftly aside and turned to face him, his eyes glittering. The pistol was pointed right at Stephen's heart. Mary cried out, as the men made no move toward the two leaders—

"What kind of men are ye, ye English? Do ye always kiss your chains and the whip that bloodies you? Fight him! Fight for your own freedom!" Her clear voice rang out in the stone cellars, the Scottish accent strong.

No one moved; the silence was deadly. Mary jumped up frantically, seeing her husband facing Basset in a deadly crouch. He would dare that pistol, pointed at his vitals—

"Ye English! Fight for your freedom!" she cried again. "No more slavery for free men! Will ye sleep always in fear, waking when someone calls ye out to obey his will? Will ye smuggle and submit to blackmail and murder? Where is your courage? Are ye English, instead, a race of cowards? Glad to be Scottish, I am, if this is to be an Englishman!"

There was muttering and growling. Some men made a move, and then paused, heavily.

A clear, hard voice rang out—Jeremiah's—and he said, "I'm with her! I'm with her. No more slavery! Come on, lads! Fight for your freedom!" And the huge man surged forward.

Someone turned to give him battle, and Jeremiah Shaw picked him up and flung him at the crowd of men, catching them all by surprise. Men cried out and turned to fight each other in a brief, bloody melee. Mary scrambled out of the way, up on the shelves, and picked up a bottle of brandy which stood to hand, half empty, as a smuggler had left it.

She watched breathlessly, over the crowd, as they fought each other. She saw Jeremiah urging on some of his friends to fight the smugglers who still sided with Evan Basset. They seemed to know, thought Mary keenly, which ones were for the smuggling and which against. Many must have been pressed reluctantly into service.

Jeremiah Shaw smashed one man against the brandy kegs, and he fell limp. Mary saw another man fighting his way to Jeremiah's side, and the two of them stood back to back against four others, and whipping them, too. Her Scottish heart beat faster at the glorious battle they were doing.

Then her attention was abruptly caught by the sight of her husband. He was closed with Basset, the two men struggling silently, scarcely moving. He was fighting for the pistol in Basset's grip, and she saw the gun wavering back and forth between the two bronzed hands.

Back and forth, pointed at the ceiling, then down, then toward one man's body, and then the other. She gasped, waiting—watching—unable to move. Men fought between her and them, but Stephen's head was high, and she could watch them in a little empty space—watch and pray and hope fiercely for her man to win—

The pistol went off. Somewhere in the darkness between their bodies, it went off. She caught her breath—held her hand to her throat, watching— If Stephen went down, and died, she died with him, she thought, and knew the strength of her love. If he died, she could no longer live.

The bodies slowly separated. She saw Stephen's hand go up wearily, slowly, to his bloody face, as he pushed the hair back, wiped his eyes, moved his head slowly. She thought he was falling and she groaned aloud.

But Basset was falling. Slowly falling, gripping himself and falling forward, his eyes going blank and sightless. Falling.

"Oh, God in heaven," whispered Mary. "God—dear God—I thank thee—"

Basset fell, and the men near them saw him and stared down incredulously. Stephen stopped and felt the pulse in his throat.

He stood up again and called in his clear voice, as he must have called after a battle on his ship, "It's over, lads. The bastard is dead! Lay down your arms and surrender!"

The heads turned toward them, the fighting hesitated, faltered. Then, with disgusted cursing, the fighters stopped and flung down their weapons—no arms, but bottles, sticks of wood, axes.

The fight was over indeed. Evan Basset and all his scheming, murderous plans were finished.

CHAPTER SIXTEEN

THE VIVID BLUE of June turned to the golden of July, and still Stephen lay sick. The wounds had become infected, and he was gravely ill for weeks. Mary nursed him devotedly, dread in her heart. She got up nights, lay on a cot near him, worried over him, scolded him when he dared stir.

Her bashfulness was forgotten. She stripped the sopping nightshirt from him when the fever wrung the moisture from his thin body. She washed him with warm water, then cool, to bring down the fever. She dressed his wounds as the doctor had instructed, scarcely sleeping many nights to care for him.

Lady Helena came often to the bedroom and sent Mary to hers, so she might care for her stepson. Only then did Mary rest, trusting the woman now as she never had before.

As soon as Christopher had heard the news, he had ridden horseback to them. He had heaped scoldings on Stephen's weak head, raging that he had missed the whole affair, infuriated that his brother had sent him away.

Lady Helena and Georgiana had followed by coach to

take up residence at the castle, though only temporarily, Georgiana said with new firmness. She had tasted the pleasure of being mistress of her own household, and would not give it up.

The family was united as never before. While Mary nursed her husband, Georgiana directed the servants. Lady Helena, with new meekness, helped them both with a gentleness which Mary could scarcely credit. And Christopher took over Stephen's duties for the time, riding out daily early and late to oversee the farms, the plantings, the problems.

And finally their work was rewarded. Stephen was able to get up for a few hours at a time. As soon as the doctor allowed, Mary moved him out to lie on a lounge in the gardens and enjoy the fresh air and the sunshine. He was so weak for a time, scarcely able to lift a limp hand, that her heart ached, and she would scold someone to hide the tears in her voice.

Bonny sang about the duties she had. Mrs. Ramsey went about with a smile and a lilt to her voice. Two of the footmen and three of the grooms had been named as conspirators helping Basset, and had been turned off. The others were loyal, said Wenrick, who seemed to have known much more than he dared say.

The countryside seemed loose from a terrible grip of fear. Mr. Ashwood the innkeeper came to talk to Mary for them all, telling her what they had known or guessed. Mr. Jones the grocer was her firm ally now, assuring her they were her servants for life for what she had done for them.

Mr. Ashwood said, "Basset built up his power for years. How could we be thinking the new lord would care what happened to us? And for all we could know, he would shrug and look the other way. It were known he served the smuggled wines at his table, smoked the smuggled tobacco. How could we be sure what his character be? But ye, Lady Mary, ye were different from the first. Ye were caring about us, and we felt, and whispered it about, that there might be changes."

"If only you could have told me," she said without reproach. "I understand your fears, but only Jeremiah Shaw dared speak."

"Aye, he be a strong man, and protects his own," said Mr. Ashwood. "But he also was threatened, and we were not knowing when he might break. Strong men we have seen, that broke under threat to their wives and children."

One mid-July day, Stephen lay in the gardens, and an old salt came to call. He came up from the village with Mr. Jones the grocer, riding on the front seat with him. He came around to the garden, his grizzled head high, his empty left sleeve swinging. But by his dark eyes, Mary knew he was uncertain of his welcome.

She went to meet the older man at the rose hedge. "Come in, Mr. Parks. You are welcome. Mr. Ashwood said you wished to see my Lord Stephen." And she smiled at him warmly and took his remaining hand in hers.

"Oh, aye," said the older man, looking ahead of her toward where Stephen lay on the lounge. "I said I would come up and speak to my captain. We fought together on the *Enterprise*, you know, ma'am—my lady, I mean."

"So I heard. Come." And she led him over to Stephen, who tried to sit up weakly.

"Nay, nay, lie back," said the grizzled salt with quick feeling. "Your wounds must be aching like mine did, a couple years ago."

"I remember you, Parks," said Stephen, smiling and holding out a weak hand. "You always fought like two demons. I was sorry when we lost you."

"No sorrier than me," he said. He finally sat down to have a talk. Mary left them to talk, and was surprised two hours later to find them still at their reminiscences. Stephen had a better color in his cheeks, and his eyes sparkled as she returned to them.

The man got up when she came. "Aye, I have overstayed my welcome," he said ruefully. "I meant to be only five minutes. It is longer than that, I think."

"You'll come again," said Stephen, and grinned up at him. "We must have another good talk. I never knew what went on that night in Lisbon. It must have been a lively fight, by the condition of the men coming aboard."

"Oh, aye, it war' a good one," he said, preparing reluctantly to leave. There was a roll in his walk as he went down the rose hedge toward the back entrance where Mr. Jones was patiently waiting with his wagon.

The word went out. Others came to call, one and two at a time, usually in the afternoon when Stephen would be in the gardens. Jeremiah Shaw came several times, uneasy at first, then more open and friendly, discussing the problems of the farmers. He seemed to be their spokesman now, thought Mary.

Some came from the village, some from the farms, some from old army or navy service, stopping by to speak a friendly word, they said. They were testing him, seeing if he would speak with them, and remained, feeling more at ease and speaking of problems and gossip.

July ended, and in August, Stephen was finally able to be up and about more. He and Christopher held long talks together, and it was decided that Christopher should return to Penhurst to manage it. Georgiana dearly wanted a house of her own to manage, said Christopher, and he appeared no less pleased at having his own acres to plan. He seemed to have new purpose and briskness in his manner.

One afternoon, they all had tea in the gardens. Stephen was sitting in a chair, firmly refusing the lounge. Mary poured, Georgiana handed around plates. Lady Helena said grandly that she would adore being waited upon, as she had spent the morning gossiping with the vicar's wife, and was thoroughly exhausted.

Georgiana dared to laugh. She had new bright color in her face, and much more assurance of manner, thought Mary. "Now, Mother, you know you love to gossip. How could it wear you out?"

Lady Helena grimaced over her teacup. "We dared to attempt to solve everyone's problems," she said ruefully. They all laughed then. "You well may laugh! It was most wearying."

"Well, we shall have a fresh set of problems at Penhurst," said Christopher teasingly, lying back lazily in his chair. "Mother, when you have all the problems solved here, you may begin at our new home. Just think what fresh solutions you might find!"

"Naughty boy," said Lady Helena fondly. "You are more like your father every day. Now Stephen takes after his mother—"

It was Mary's turn to laugh. They all turned to gaze at her. "He is not like his mother," she said spiritedly. "He is the image of his father, just as stubborn and opinionated, and domineering, and strong." Then she colored richly, and bent her head over the teapot at Stephen's amused look.

"You may be right, dear," said Lady Helena, unexpectedly, nodding her gray-blonde head. "The way he sent us off without a word of explanation! It quite broke my heart that he should be so cold and abrupt. I should have known he was like his father, thinking of us rather than of himself."

"I cannot find it in my heart to forgive you, Stephen," said Christopher, stretching out his long legs. "I missed a bully fight! If I had been here, you might not have gotten those wounds, you know!"

"Ah, but I had my fine fighting Scottish wife by my side," said Stephen teasingly at Mary, smiling over at her bent head. She glanced up, caught the smile, blushed, and looked away. "You should have heard her rallying the men! It was grand. If I had had her as mate on my ship, we should have won all the battles in half the time!"

"Mary is a strong one," said Lady Helena. "You picked the right wife for you, Stephen. You would never have been satisfied with a weak, meek wife."

"Ah, but I mean to tame her," he said coolly. "She is still too stubborn for my taste!"

Mary was flushing wildly by that time. Lady Helena's unexpected praise had flustered her, Stephen's veiled threat held prospects for the future about which she had not dared to think.

They had not spoken intimately together since before her hasty departure from the castle. They had not slept together at all. He had been too ill to make any demands on her but those for his health.

What did he really feel about her? The last time they had spoken frankly, she had accused him of being weary of her, and he had not denied it. The color died in her face, and she felt suddenly tired and uncertain.

Georgiana, with new tact and poise, changed the subject and discussed some of the problems of Penhurst with Stephen and Christopher. Mary listened silently, thinking how changed all of their situations had become. They seemed—friendly. Frank. As though they had each found their place in life and could talk as allies rather than enemies.

"Do you mean to hire a new overseer?" Christopher asked presently. "Basset did do a huge job; I don't see how one man can manage it all. And there are still some distant properties."

Stephen grimaced. "It will be a time before I can trust any man again for that," he said with distaste.

Lady Helena said thoughtfully, "The son of a friend of mine, Lord Cardriff, is selling out his commission. He is a most efficient man and longs to go on the land. He lost a leg, you know. I wonder if he might consider—he is a man of honor, though no money—"

"Hum, Cardriff. I had not thought of him," said Stephen, musing. "The grandfather lost their money in gambling, I believe. I wonder if the boy is like him."

"Not a bit of it," said Christopher. "Won't touch cards, proud as Lucifer. Knew him when we went up together. I'd vouch for him, Stephen."

"I'll have him over for a talk. He is interested in the land, then?"

"Mad keen on it. Always off hunting and fishing, testing the soil with his fingers, that bit," said Christopher. "Thought I'd have him over to look at the land that borders on the sea at Penhurst. He might be able to suggest something."

They discussed the matter in friendly fashion. Finally tea was over, and the others went inside to go about their varied interests. Mary saw the tea table wheeled away by the footman, and got up to look at the rose hedges.

"Where are you going, Mary?" asked Stephen from his seat.

"The roses. I think the white ones should be replanted next year. The gardener said—"

"Come here, Mary."

She paused and turned back startled, staring at him. Why did he use that tone to her, that officious, commanding tone?

She did not come a step. "Is your head bothering you, Stephen? I thought the wound was healing, but I could get some fresh ointment—"

"Come here, Mary," he said again, more coldly, frowning.

She bit her lips. "What do you want?"

"Mary, if I have to order you again, I shall make you sorry!"

She scowled at him, came a reluctant step to him, another, another. He held out his hand imperiously to her. Finally she came close enough to put her hand in his. He held her hand tightly, pulled her closer. She stood beside his chair, looking down at him.

"Still stubborn, my Mary?" he asked softly. "When are you going to learn to obey me at once?"

She looked at him to see if he were teasing. She was not sure. She eyed him doubtfully. With a sudden movement, he pulled her down onto his knees. She gasped, tried to get up. He wrapped his arms about her strongly.

"Sit still. I want to talk to you. Whenever I begin to talk, you are always off and about another ridiculous errand. No, I won't let you go! Sit still!"

"You will hurt your shoulder," she said, twisting about so he could not hold her quite so tightly against him. Her heart was thumping.

"I want to have a talk with you," he said more quietly, holding her closely against him. He turned her a little more so he could look down into her face. She bent her head. "Look at me, Mary. That day—when I told you to leave the castle and go to London, you gave in at once. Why?"

"Why—sir?" she asked feebly. "You told me—"

"You never obey my orders so rapidly," he said ironically, a half-cynical smile on his lips. "So why did you go? I anticipated a long argument. Instead, you gave in at once and went off to London to get a divorce—just as I bade you! Why, Mary?"

She remembered that day vividly. She sat thinking about it, the pain flooding her once more. The misery when she realized he was abruptly weary of her, sick of her, through with her.

"Why, Mary?" he asked again, half-shaking her.

She turned, glanced once into the sherry-bright eyes, and flinched away. "Well—sir—," she said uncertainly.

"I thought—I felt—I mean—ye were weary of me—and I was not one to say when someone—was weary—of me—"

"I was weary of you?" he asked softly, his arms almost cruelly tight. "Who said I was weary of you?"

"Ye did!" she said with spirit. "Ye said ye were—tired of me—weary of me—finished—"

"I never said that. You asked a question, and I said you may well think so. I did not say I was weary of you. Mary, did it grieve you to think I meant it?"

She was silent, turning her head away from him, flushing and paling by turns. He gave her an impatient little shake.

"My Mary, I love you. Do you have to be spanked and scolded and harrassed into saying you love me too? Is that it? Must I spank you? Or shall I kiss you to pieces, until you lie in my arms and your face softens as it does when I make love to you, and you melt into me and love me in return? Must I?"

Her breath was catching in surprise, and she turned her face into his shoulder, her hands clutching at the tight arms about her. "Ye don't," she said, muffled.

"I don't what? Have to make love to you to make you confess your love?" he asked in her ear, then kissed the white neck below in a hard, passionate kiss. "Mary—tell me. Tell me you love me, or I shall make love to you right now, out in the gardens, in plain sight of all who care to look out the windows! I am weary of your evading me! Tell me—or—"

"Do ye—love me?" she whispered, winding her arms about his neck. She could not believe it, it could not be true, though her heart was beating wildly next to his.

"Tell me first," he ordered imperiously, turning her face up to his from its hiding place. There was a slight, triumphant smile on the large mouth which had kissed hers often—but never enough. "Tell me—at once!"

"I—love—you—Stephen," she finally whispered. His

mouth crushed down on hers, almost blurring the confession.

"There. I thought you would never say it. What a stubborn wife I have, to be sure! Mary, I loved you from the first day, when I looked up to see you in the doorway of my study. You, with your weary face and tired eyes and mussed red hair—and your stubborn Scottish chin up high and your little fists clenched—I loved you at once. A girl of spirit and will and intelligence, and such a sweet darling love—" He was whispering the words against her lips between kisses.

"Oh—ye did not! Ye did not love—me—at first—ye were hard and cold—," she managed to protest. "Ye did not—love me—at all—ye were brutal—"

"Now, you are defying me all over again. How am I going to tame you?" he teased, and she heard the hard beat of his heart, and felt it against her breasts as he crushed her close. "I know only one way to conquer you—and I shall do it, my love!"

"How is that?" she asked, with one last defiant toss of her head.

He laughed and leaned to whisper in her ears just how he meant to conquer her. But his arms were now tender, and held her with care, and she rested happily against the heart which beat truly for her, she knew now.

How wonderful it was, they both thought, to be so happy after so many trials.